One White Lie

Barrington Billionaire Series

Book One

by
Jeannette Winters

Author Contact
website: JeannetteWinters.com
email: authorjeannettewinters@gmail.com
Facebook: Author Jeannette Winters
Twitter: @JWintersAuthor

Brice Henderson traded everything for power and success. His company was closing a deal that would cement his spot at the top. The last thing he needed was a distraction from the past.

Lena Razzi had spent years trying to forget Brice Henderson. When offered the opportunity of a lifetime, would she take the risk even if the price would be another broken heart?

Do you love reading from this world? Continue with Always Mine from my sister, Ruth Cardello, and Fierce Love from my niece Danielle Stewart Their series will mirror my time line. It isn't necessary to read theirs to enjoy mine, but it sure will enhance the fun!

Copyright

Dedication

This book is dedicated to my brothers who continue to ask me about my books even though I know they really don't want to hear the details. Thanks for always being there.

I am also supported by a team of beta readers who aren't afraid to tell me the truth. Thank you for that!

Karen Lawson, Janet Hitchcock, E.L. King and Marion Arche, my editors as well as Nicole Sanders at Trevino Creative Graphic Design for my cover, you are all amazing!

And to my co-workers, you all know who you are. Your endless support and cheering on is so appreciated!

To my readers who brings joy into my life with each and every message. *Always keep romance in your lives!*

Chapter One

FILLED WITH FRUSTRATION, Brice Henderson slammed the phone down as he leaned back in his chair. *No way.* There were times a partner came in handy, but, for the most part, it meant only another opinion he didn't want to hear. Asher Barrington could put whatever deadline he wanted on the project, but no one was going to tell him what he had to do or when he had to do it. Not in his company or any other part of his life. *Those days are long gone.*

Asher didn't get it. *A highly sensitive chemical compound is not something you can rush. One mistake and . . .*

He didn't want to even think about the consequences; they would be catastrophic. *No one is pushing me into supplying a deficient product.* That thought alone brought back the last time he had seen his father. It had been more than three years ago and had ended with one hell of an argument around this very issue. "Stop this project now or consider yourself unemployed." In that moment, he'd thought his father was a controlling asshole who wouldn't even take the time to listen to what this project could mean for them as a family. *Always his way or the highway.* Asher Barrington reminded him of his father at times. Only one way, his way, drive forward as hard as you can, and if something is in the way, crush it. The decision to walk away from the family business hadn't been an easy one. As the eldest, his siblings assumed he would eventually take over the business. It was lucrative, but he could see the writing on the wall. His father's investments were working now, but times were changing, and Brice wasn't going to get caught behind the eight ball.

Too many years had been spent in his father's shadow, and for what? To be given the same treatment as any other employee and at times even worse? The days of being under his father's thumb were long over. Never would Brice allow himself to lose focus on all that mattered to him again. *My dreams, my future.*

Although that argument was in the past, Brice hadn't wasted or regretted one moment of it. Hell would freeze over before he went back to his father, asking for his old job back. It didn't matter how much time it took; his name was on this project, and there was no way he was going to deliver a substandard product. If that meant his staff had no social life, so be it. Each one of them knew what they were in for when they chose to leave Poly-Shyn and work for him. Yes, he was demanding and what some may call arrogant, but they were all paid extremely well, so as far as he was concerned, they had no right to complain. He wanted and expected one thing from them. *Results.*

For the most part, he could count on each of them to do their job and do it well. There was only one problem. His personal assistant, Nancy, informed him she needed to take emergency family leave to care for her sickly mother. The look on her face when he'd suggested yesterday that he would be willing to pay for a nurse so she could continue working was one he had never seen before from her. "Some things are more important than a job or money. I only hope you realize that before it's too late and you're left with only your regrets to keep you company at night." Her words had echoed through him all day. However, the outcome hadn't changed. On an ordinary day, she was an important part of his team, but at this critical time, she was invaluable. Nancy had a shrewd way of handling the day-to-day mayhem and only directed something to him that truly needed his attention. With her out for an extended period, he had no idea what bullshit was about to fall into his lap, and right now he had no time to deal with any of it.

Getting up from his desk, he headed out of the office. Between Asher and Nancy, these next few weeks were going to be hell. *I need the answer now.* Nancy looked sweet and innocent, but he knew she was as tough as nails. There were times he was grateful she had the courage to challenge him. But right now wasn't one of those times.

"You better have good news for me," Brice bellowed.

Nancy raised her eyes from her computer screen

without even a blink of an eye, as she responded, "You gave very specific instructions about the skills my temporary replacement needed to possess."

"And after all these years you should know by now they are non-negotiable."

Shaking her head, Nancy added, "Then you should remember I have never let you down before."

He didn't respond, only glared at her. *She was right. As usual.* Nancy knew he trusted her. Otherwise, he would never have let her interview and hire someone without even meeting her replacement. Even though she was correct, if she was looking for praise for doing her job, she wasn't going to get it from him. "So when can I expect her?" *And she better damn well be good.*

A small grin appeared on her face as she answered, "She'll be here first thing tomorrow morning." Brice opened his mouth to say something, but Nancy raised her hand to cut him off. "Before you say it, I have researched her background, performed an extensive interview, and have already prepared clear and concise instructions. She also has my cell phone number for any emergencies, and yes, I have informed her you are not to be interrupted under any circumstances whatsoever."

And this is precisely why I need you to stay. Brice didn't have any time to waste trying to convince her to change her mind. All he could do was trust that she'd hired the right person for the job. It was a gamble, and he was the one with a lot to lose if she didn't work out. *I don't have any choice.* "You'll be hearing from me if she can't do everything I requested, and you'll need to get your ass back to work."

"Brice, you won't be disappointed with this one. I guarantee it. I'm more worried that you won't want me back after my mother—" Nancy stopped herself from saying more, the words too difficult to say.

It was the first time he had seen her anything other than confident. There was nothing he could say to change what she was going through. In a much softer tone he said, "Your job will be here." She smiled and nodded her thanks. Before Nancy became emotional, he left her desk and headed for the elevator. Calling over his shoulder, he said to her, "I'll be in the lab if anything urgent comes up."

He needed everyone to be on top of their game. The formula was nearly perfect, and some of his team mistakenly thought that was close enough. Over the next few weeks, he was sure they were going to regret ever saying those words to him. *I won't tolerate any incompetence in this company. Mine or anyone else's.*

Once he entered the lab, he went into the office and shut his door. There wasn't time for interruptions or small talk with the chemist. With Asher moving up the timetable, he wanted to make sure everyone was giving one hundred fifty percent. He had risked everything, and nothing or no one was going to get in the way of seeing his vision become a reality.

LENA RAZZI COULDN'T believe she was going to be late

for the first day of her new temp job. She'd had many of them in the past but normally got to meet the boss or staff in person prior to accepting the position. Even the interview had been handled over the phone. If it was going to be a long-term assignment or permanent position she probably wouldn't have taken the job because she didn't want to work for someone who couldn't even take five minutes to meet her. But since this wasn't going to last forever, she didn't have much to lose. *I can put up with anything for a month. I've worked for difficult bosses longer than this for less money. How bad can Mr. Henderson be? He's clearly a very busy man, which suits me because I also prefer to be busy.*

Although her phone interview was extensive, there were a few things Nancy had stressed more than once. The top of the list was to make sure Mr. Henderson had his coffee and clean towels ready and waiting for him when he came in from his early morning run. *Running late was not going to be a great first impression. But my first impression of my new boss isn't so great either.*

Maybe if she explained what happened with her son, Nicholas, on his first day at daycare, it would help. *He decided it was the perfect time to have a meltdown and didn't want Mommy to leave. It was so unlike him.* Normally he was a bundle of joy, all smiles, and loving everyone. *Today, not so much.* All she could do was hope Mr. Henderson liked children and understood her plight. *He's probably a cranky old man who hates them, and his run is probably a walk around the block.*

Rushing into the office building the security guard stopped her.

"Hi. I'm Lena Razzi, Nancy's temporary replacement. I was told to report to the ninth floor."

He looked her over and said, "We need to take your picture for your badge."

Not now. I'm late enough already. "Okay. Let me take care of a few things for Mr. Henderson, and I will return shortly."

The man shook his head. "This is a secure facility. You cannot access the elevator without your badge. It will only take a few minutes. Follow me, please."

Lena wondered what else Nancy may have failed to inform her about this company. *I really should have asked more questions.* The only reason she hadn't was it had been an opportunity too good to pass up. Forcing a fake smile, she did as he said. *At least I will have a valid reason for being late.* Within minutes, she had her badge and was riding the elevator to her new office. She looked at her picture and was horrified. *That camera takes horrible pictures.* She had taken the time to apply her makeup perfectly this morning before Nicholas had even woken. The picture, however, didn't reflect that. Opening her purse, she pulled out a compact mirror, and to her horror, it wasn't the camera after all. *Nicholas, I guess you weren't the only one having a hard time saying goodbye this morning.* Anyone looking at her now would think she had been out all night drinking and hadn't made it home yet. Her eyes were puffy and bloodshot. Her mascara was ruined and the elegant light hint of blush she applied was now streaked. *Can my morning get any worse?* She couldn't believe this was happening.

Digging through her bag, she found many items, none of which were going to fix the issues at hand. Without makeup in her bag, the best thing she could do was remove as much as she could. Lena contemplated spitting on a tissue to wipe it off when she remembered her emergency pack of baby wipes. Opening the packet, she was relieved to find one left. She ran it over her face the best she could. Looking back into the mirror she was thankful for the improvement, but nothing fixed her eyes. *Maybe he'll be in a meeting, and I won't even see him today.* Nancy had said he spent most of his time in the lab. *Please let this be one of those days.*

As the elevator doors opened, she stood as confidently as she could muster—head held high—and headed to the end of the hall where Nancy had said she would find her desk ready and waiting for her. What had she been thinking to take on a job like this? She had all the skills needed to do the job and to be great at it, but she was a single mother of a two-and-a-half-year-old boy. And there lay her answer. She was doing this for Nicholas. The money she had in savings before she gave birth was quickly diminishing. With her student loans, rent, and basic necessities, she had no choice other than to take this job and make it work. Besides, it paid her weekly what other jobs paid for an entire month. No matter what, even if he yelled, screamed, or worked her to the bone, she had to remind herself this wasn't about her. This job was all about Nicholas, and there wasn't anything she wouldn't do for him.

There were times she thought about reaching out to his father for monetary help, but he had made it very clear he wanted no children or family. She wasn't going to expose her son to that type of rejection twice. *I can and will do this.* Putting her purse in the desk drawer, she headed for the closed office door near her. *Really, how bad can it be? It's only going to be for one month.* Lena knocked softly. *Please don't be here yet.*

"You're late," a deep voice barked from the other side of the door. Before she could answer, the door was pulled open, leaving her face to face with her new boss.

Brice! Brice Henderson? *How? Why? Doesn't he work for his father?* Everything in her said turn, run, but instead she stood there frozen, unable to move or speak. As her initial shock wore off, it was replaced by anger. Her pulse was racing. It had been three years since she had seen him and the last time he had broken her heart. It had taken a long time to get her life back on track, to stop wondering or caring what she had said or had done to make him break it off so abruptly. Now, here he stood with a look of contempt on his face. If anyone should be pissed off at this situation, it should be her. His eyes fixed on hers. Lena turned her face slightly to avoid the direct contact. *I've never been good at hiding my emotions.* That was a different time; she wasn't the same person any longer.

"Lena. What are you doing here?" he asked sharply.

Give me strength. And lots of it. "I'm your assistant—temporarily, that is." She could feel his cool gray eyes look her up and down as though he hoped they were playing tricks on him. It was evident she was the last person he wanted to see at his door. *Yeah, you're not my first choice either.*

"Hell, no."

Her mouth gaped open in amazement at his boldness. Then she remembered all too well *who* she was talking to. *Nothing you say should surprise me anymore.* Lena wasn't about to back down, not from him or anyone else. If he expected her to be the soft and sweet girl he'd dated, he was going to be sadly mistaken. *That girl no longer exists, thanks to you.* "Good morning to you as well, Mr. Henderson."

If he picked up on her sarcasm, he didn't let it show. Without even blinking, in a firm tone he said, "We're not doing this."

She wasn't sure what he meant. If he thought she had planned this, that she knew he was the Mr. Henderson she was going to report to, then he couldn't be further from the truth. *It's such a common name. He's the last person I expected to see.* In fact, if she'd had any indication who her new boss was going to be, she wouldn't have accepted the position. *God, he was still as handsome as hell, but when did he become so mean?* Maybe she'd been blinded by love back then and hadn't noticed. Whatever, it was no longer her concern. There was only one thing she was here for, and that was the hefty paycheck that came with this title. "A lot has changed since the last time we spoke. I can assure you, Mr. Henderson, I have the qualifications to do this job. If I didn't, your assistant wouldn't have offered me this position." She met his gaze and added, "Unless you don't trust her judgment."

Brice's nostrils flared. "Don't concern yourself with whom I do or don't trust. There is no way I can have you working in my office."

Panic filled her. "Why?"

"Not that I owe you an explanation, but our history would be at the top of the list," he said plainly.

No shit. That totally slipped my mind. How badly she wanted to tell him exactly what she thought of him and what he could do with this job, but wasn't going to keep a roof over Nicholas's head. No, she needed to suck it up and do the only thing a person in this situation could do. *Plead.* "Bri . . . I mean, Mr. Henderson, Nancy explained that you are in a crucial phase of your project. Please give me one week to show you I can do this."

"No."

Damn, he isn't going to make this easy. "Okay, the truth is, I honestly need this job. My school loans are due, and I have rent to pay. I turned down another opportunity for this job. If you turn me away now, I won't be able to pay my bills." In a more controlled tone she said, "What we had was a long time ago. It won't affect my performance now unless you're concerned it will affect yours."

The room fell into an uncomfortable silence. Looking at her intensely he said, "Nothing will interfere with my success. Not you or anyone else. Do I make myself clear?"

Crystal. Nodding, she said, "Understood." There was so much she wanted to say; she understood because she felt the same about providing a good stable home for Nicholas. Pushing the topic would only fuel his original opinion that they couldn't work together. *Less is more.* Lena turned her focus back to her assignment. Trying not to show any emotion, she asked, "So may I get you a cup of coffee?"

It was sad to think that Nicholas's and her future completely rested on Brice's need of caffeine fix. *Please be thirsty.* She had spent the last three years avoiding any form of drama, and she was now trying to sweet talk her way right back into it. *Remember, this is for Nicholas.*

Chapter Two

THE LAST THING he needed right now was an ex-lover creeping into his life. Brice wanted to tell her to get out of his office, that it didn't matter to him if she ended up on the street, but he knew that was a lie. He'd always been attracted to Lena in a way that was unlike any other. That was the problem back then, and apparently it hadn't lessened over the years. *Why you, Lena?* Being in the same building, never mind his office, was going to bring a whole new level of distraction into his life. *I don't have time for this shit.*

B&H Advanced Engineering was his company. He made the decisions, not some Human Resources department telling him what he could or couldn't do. So why was she still there? *Because, you spicy thing, you challenged me, and I never walk away from a challenge.* He watched her turn away and head off to make his coffee. Was it his imagination or had he seen a slight curl of her lips before she left? *Lena being here isn't good.* No matter how he tried to resist, he found himself checking out the curve of her hips as she swayed, teasing him. *You were sexy before, but damn, you filled out nicely.* His blood grew warm with need. Running his hands through his hair in frustration, he slammed the door. *Out of sight, out of mind.*

That may have worked for the last three years, but somehow he didn't think it was going to be quite that easy now. *What are the odds with all the people in Boston, you show up at my door, Lena?* Something didn't feel right. Could this truly be a coincidence or was this some form of payback from Nancy for giving her grief about taking a medical leave when he needed her most? *No, she wouldn't, would she?* Yesterday he would've said no. When he and Lena were dating, Nancy was his father's assistant, not his, so she wouldn't have information regarding his personal life. Then again, could she have overheard one of the many arguments he'd had with his father about his choice in women? Nancy did have an uncanny memory for details that most people overlooked. It wouldn't surprise him one bit if she'd held on to that information for when she needed it most. *Well played, Nancy.* If it weren't for the fact that she was his right hand in running this business, she should consider herself fired. *I won't forget this when you return.*

He needed someone on the front line to deter the endless interruptions that Nancy handled so effortlessly. She might not have been thrilled with his lack of empathy, but there was still no way Nancy would've hired Lena if she, in fact, hadn't had the skills needed to do the job. And do the job to his satisfaction. *A lot has changed. I can make this work.* Brice knew the risk if it didn't. He hadn't spent every waking moment for the last three years practically hibernating in his office and lab to have Lena Razzi crash-land back into his life and ruin the goals he had set for himself.

I hope I don't regret this. Brice tossed his cell phone on the leather couch, and headed for the shower. As he turned the water on, he couldn't get the picture of her olive skin and deep brown eyes out of his mind. A cold one was in order.

HER HANDS TREMBLED as she poured his coffee. *Brice.* His name continued to echo in her mind over and over again. *What did I get myself into?* The situation was no longer about whether she had the skills for the job. It was about finding a way to be around Brice Henderson on a daily basis and not allow what they once shared to affect her life in any way.

The last time she saw him was a day she'd worked hard to forget. For the most part, it had become a blur, a moment in time that had begun to fade away. Seeing him now brought it all back as though it were yesterday. They had been dating for a year, and everything seemed to be going great. Neither of them had spoken of the future, yet she'd felt hopeful. At that time, she would have shouted from the rooftop how much she loved the man. Would have done anything for him. In a blink of an eye, that all vanished. They were supposed to meet for dinner that night, and she had bought a new dress for the occasion. There was something huge she needed to talk to him about, but the opportunity never came. Harsh words crushed their little romantic evening. When Brice arrived to pick her up, she could sense his anger. His jaw had been tense, and his hands had been clenched into a fist as though itching for a fight. When Lena suggested maybe they should make it another night, he flew off the handle, yelling things that still to this day made no sense. He accused her of trying to hold him back from achieving his dreams. She had been so shocked and stunned, she could only stand there, her mouth gaping wide open. Lena had thought his dream was to one day take over the family business, but he had always kept his work life private. Had he wanted her to ask, to have been more involved? With the benefit of hindsight, he must have since her original tactic hadn't been enough. Back then she thought the best way to keep him happy was to discuss only positive things, not how his day never appeared to be that. Thinking back now, maybe he'd wanted her to ask. *Maybe he'd needed me to ask.* Maybe if she had spoken up then his words and actions wouldn't have been such a surprise. Brice had been ranting and raving about some project and how it was the answer to all his problems. Before she could ask him to explain, he had turned to her and said sharply, "No one, including my family or you, will ever come between me and achieving my dreams. That's the one and only thing that's important to me. The success of this project is my life." Lena never heard from Brice again after that horrible night. He had made no further contact and had obviously completely forgotten about her and moved on. She hadn't seen him since that night. *Until now.*

Stirring the coffee reminded her of the last morning they'd woken in each other's arms. How had she been so foolish to have believed he could've been her happily ever after? It wasn't just Brice who had moved on with his life, so had she. She wanted to hate him, but she couldn't. Because of him she'd found the most important thing in her life. *Nicholas.* There was only one major problem; she hadn't shared his existence with Brice that night, and hence, he still didn't know. *And I'm going to keep it that way. Nicholas doesn't need to be anything less than what he is: wanted.*

Keeping her work and personal life separate was now imperative. *I just hope it's not impossible. You were my first love, Brice, but you no longer hold that position.*

Chapter Three

LENA'S INITIAL FEAR of seeing Brice more than she could handle faded after a few days. The only time she saw him was when he grabbed his coffee each morning on the way to the lab and even then no words were spoken.

Not having to interact with him was what she wanted, and she should be happy with that. Instead, it somehow only added to her anger. *Never seeing you again was definitely what I wanted, but come on, Brice, would it kill you to at least acknowledge my presence?*

Thankfully the continuous ringing of the phone kept her busy throughout the day. It was amusing how persistent people were. At what point would they get the hint that Mr. Henderson was never going to take their call? *It would be so much easier if I were allowed to tell them that straight up.*

If it weren't for the fact Nancy had given her the "okay to transfer call" list, Lena would have thought Brice blew off everyone. *I know which list I'd be on.*

Picking up the receiver for the hundredth time that

day, she said, "Good afternoon, Mr. Henderson's office. This is Lena, how may I help you?"

"So how is your first week? Have you found everything?" Nancy asked.

Oh, if you only knew. "Yes. Things are just as you described. Thank you for leaving such detailed notes."

"I'm glad you're enjoying the position."

You couldn't be further from the truth. "I have settled in fine."

"Good. I was worried you might find it . . . difficult."

Oh, you don't know the half of it. Difficult is the understatement of the year. Lena asked a few brief questions regarding billing and ordering supplies. Nancy rattled off the answers without hesitation. She ran a tight ship and left everything in such good order it didn't leave room for error. With the few business items off the table, Lena tried to change the subject before Nancy asked how she and Brice were getting along. It wasn't what Lena should say that concerned her as much as it was what she would say. Somehow when she thought of him, her mouth spewed words without a filter. The last thing she needed was Nancy second-guessing if she had made the right choice hiring her. "How is your mother doing?"

A short pause and Nancy's voice wasn't as happy when she responded. "I'm glad I took the time to be with her."

Why the hell did I ask that? Even though the relationship with her parents was not picture-perfect, at least they both were healthy. *Not something I should take for granted either.* Just hearing the strain in Nancy's voice made Lena want to call her mother and tell her how much she loved her, appreciated her. Ever since she declared she was keeping the baby and would never again speak the name of the father, they'd spoken, but with forced pleasantries. *Maybe we start with a visit back home first.* "Don't worry about things here. I have your number and won't be shy. I'll call you if I have any questions."

"I knew the moment Talent Hunters sent me your résumé you were perfect for the job. What concerns I may have had at first are now gone. You don't know how relieved I am to hear things are going well. It will give me the ability to focus on what I need to do here." Nancy chuckled.

Lena had been surprised how quickly everything had moved. First Talent Hunters Agency called her and asked for her résumé, and then that same afternoon they scheduled the phone interview with Nancy for two days later. At the time she thought it was fate, that her struggle was almost over, and her luck had finally turned. *Was I far from the bullseye or what?*

It was too late now and from their brief phone call, things seemed worse than Nancy may have at first anticipated. *Just what I need. Another reason I can't walk out that door and never show up again.* This month was going to be the longest ever. *Just keep your distance, Brice, and all will be good.*

No matter how angry or hurt she had been, thoughts

of how wonderful it had been before their breakup started to creep back into her mind. She had pictured them growing old together. No one had ever made her feel loved and so special. *And then in an instant, you made me feel worthless, disposable.* She wasn't sure it was something she could ever forget because the moment she did, she risked it happening all over again. *Hurt me once, shame on you; hurt me twice, shame on me.*

Five thirty. *Another day over.* Pulling her purse out of the desk drawer, she straightened her desk and headed out of the office. This job was an opportunity to prove herself as a highly skilled personal assistant. When she and Nancy had first spoken about it, she had crossed her fingers with the hope that if she could make them see how capable she was, maybe a full-time permanent position would be available to her. However, she would mark each day off with a large X and slowly count them down. *There's nothing here for me after Nancy returns.*

She hated leaving work after the sun had already set, but at least the daylight hours were getting longer and things were changing. Most days, Lena enjoyed the diversity of seasons New England had to offer, spring and fall being her favorites. She even had found it peaceful walking at night as the snowflakes fell, leaving everything so clean and white, but with that came the frigid temperatures. I *can't wait until this freezing winter weather is over.* There was nothing enjoyable about it right now. Maneuvering within the snowbound and icy city with someone who couldn't decide if they wanted up or down made everything more work. *Maybe after this job I should move back home to Plymouth.* It would be a much quieter place to raise her son, and she knew her parents would be happy too. *Everyone's happy, except for me.* Going home would be like admitting they were right; she couldn't make it alone in Boston. There was no way was she going to admit to them or to herself that she failed.

Making her way through the noisy streets, Lena rushed to pick up her son before the daycare closed at six. With only a few minutes to spare she entered the door to see her son was the last one to be picked up. *Just a few more weeks, Nicholas, then back to normal.* She bundled him up, and they went out into the night. It was going to be good to get home for some quality mommy time before a bath and bedtime. Thankfully this job didn't require any overtime as it was already tough enough having him at daycare so long. The last thing she wanted to do was ask one of her friends to pick him up and watch him at night. *No amount of money is worth me not being there for him.*

IT HAD NEVER bothered Brice to spend extra long hours in the lab. He was the first to arrive, the last to leave, and only stopped because he needed to eat. That lifestyle appealed to him because the more he worked, the closer he was to achieving the success he desired.

The moment he saw Lena standing at his office door, his nights were no longer filled with thoughts of calculations and chemical compounds. He was once again being haunted by memories of the long nights they had spent lying naked, enjoying what each other had to offer. When they made love, she had been so responsive to him. Would she be so now? He could almost hear the soft purr she made as he made her come.

Slamming his fist onto the desk, he tried to focus on the monitor in front of him. *Damn you, Brice. Concentrate.* Even though he only saw her a few seconds a day, it was enough to throw off his entire game. Was she purposely trying to distract him by seeming uninterested? If Lena thought he hadn't noticed her watching him as he walked away from her desk, she was wrong. He didn't miss a thing about her. He never had. It was written all over her beautiful face. *She still wants me, and fuck, I still want her.*

Any other time and any other woman, he would have been more than happy to fulfill her desires and his as well. But this wasn't the time for even the simplest distraction, never mind one as sweet as her. No matter how badly he wanted to take her into his office, rip off the blouse covering her full breasts, and taste every inch of them, it would need to wait. *Just a few more weeks and everything will be just like I have dreamed.* Everything he'd worked so hard for was about to become reality, and future possibilities were limitless. No way was he going to blow it lusting after a woman, no matter how badly he wanted her. He needed to keep his priorities straight. Like any professional sportsman, you chill out before the big game, and his was just about to begin. The difference was, this was a once in a lifetime opportunity. If he blew it, there was no second chance. Everything he had given up, including Lena, would've been for nothing.

Chapter Four

LENA HAD BEEN up most of the night with Nicholas, who had a low-grade fever. Unfortunately, while being up with Nicholas, she instinctively did what most new parents do: she called her mother on FaceTime and asked for advice. She was sure she knew what the issue was but found comfort in hearing it from someone else. Her mother said, "You spiked a fever with every tooth you cut at that same age. If we had a dollar for every sleepless night with you kids, I think we could've retired at age forty."

Lena hadn't given her parents any cause to worry throughout her teenage years, at least nothing like her brothers had. Her brothers teased her about always trying to be perfect, never making a mistake. *Boy did that all change when I became a single parent.* If she had let them know who she had been dating, she was positive her brothers would have searched out Nicholas's father and demanded a wedding. *That would have been worse than doing this on my own. Being with someone who didn't want me, didn't want us.*

She spent more than an hour on FaceTime, and Nicholas didn't want to give up the phone. Even her mother seemed to be enjoying herself, especially when Nicholas called her Nana. It even melted Lena's heart hearing her son say it for the first time. Before they hung up, Lena found herself agreeing to spend the weekend. Now, on little to no sleep, she wished she had declined the offer last night. *If I call now, they will only think I am avoiding going. They'd be right.*

At least it was Friday, and when she picked Nicholas up later, they could spend the entire weekend catching up on the precious time they'd missed. After finally convincing him the grape Tylenol was yummy, she bundled him up in his hat, scarf, and mittens. On top of everything else, the weatherman decided to break the bad news that morning, saying it was going to be the coldest day of the year. *This day has to get better.*

Once outside she quickly hustled to the bus stop. She was already thinking spring when the coldest day of the season hit. *Really? It's the last day of February. I am so done with winter already.* On any other day, she would have kept distance between her and the crowd of passengers waiting to board. Today she found comfort in being surrounded by a mass of people huddled together. *At least they make a great wind barrier.* Pulling the blanket up around Nicholas to block the remaining wind, she stood amongst the noise of the early morning street traffic. *I need to win the lottery.*

When the bus finally arrived, what was once comforting, she now found to be rude. People bumped and pushed their way past her to board. *Hello, you idiots, don't you see I have a child in my arms?* Most days she felt invisible, so why should today be any different? *Maybe because I need it to be.*

On days like this she wished she had someone to lean on for emotional support. Yes, she had friends, but none of them had children. When they were dragging themselves to work after no sleep, it was from a party the night before or from hooking up with some sexy hunk. It seemed like it had been ages that she'd done either. The last time had been . . . *Don't think about it, Lena. It's all in the past. Keep it there.*

That was easier said than done. Even though she didn't see Brice often, just being in the same building brought challenges. *Like his cologne that lingered in the air after he walked away.* She couldn't believe he still wore it. Lena had purchased a bottle of Polo for him when they were shopping one day because the blend of the cologne and his natural scent drove her wild. *I couldn't resist it then and still can't.* Some things hadn't changed. *God, you smell divine.* What she didn't understand was, despite his obvious wealth, he still wore it. He could afford whatever he wanted, so why wear that? *Does he wear it because it reminds him of me?* That knowledge was bittersweet. There was a huge part of her that hoped he had some regrets and was tortured by sweet memories of their time together, but she didn't see him losing sleep over her. Not after the cold way he broke everything off. No, he probably wore it because finding a new brand wasn't important to him. That was how he functioned, after all.

Anger was building within her. The last thing she wanted to do was spend even a second of her time thinking about him and why he did things the way he did. *He doesn't mean anything to me.* She was trying to brush the memories from her mind. *Not anymore.*

The bus doors opened, and she made her way down to the subway with her son still sleeping in her arms. Nothing ever seemed to faze him, not the loud noises or bright lights. He was not like her at all. Lena was easily distracted and always had been. Even now she couldn't bake cookies and watch television. She would become absorbed in the show until the blaring smoke detector snapped her back to the task at hand. Yet oddly when she was with her son, nothing and no one broke her focus. Since having Nicholas, she had changed so much. She was no longer living just for herself. Another person's well-being came before her own.

Just another difference between us, Brice. You easily walked away. I could never do that. Not for all the money in the world. She still couldn't believe Brice's father was on the "do not transfer call" list. Even though they'd dated for a year, she'd only met his father once, and that was one time too many. He looked at her like someone would look over a car they were thinking about purchasing then decide the car wasn't worth it. It had been apparent he hadn't approved of her for his son, and she hadn't cared. Brice hadn't appeared to be anything like his father. *Maybe I was wrong.*

Lena had met Brice's younger sister, Zoey, a few times and once they even double-dated. It had been a total flop. The guy she was dating had tattoos covering every visible inch of his body. She had no issue with that except that throughout dinner he wanted to show more of them to her and had taken off his shirt. Lena felt so sad for Zoey because Brice had grabbed her date and physically removed him from the restaurant before the manager could. When Zoey had opened her mouth to protest Brice stopped her saying, "Date who you want, but don't bring them around me." That was their first and last double date.

Funny, Zoey was the only name she recognized on Nancy's call list of people Brice would answer. *At least she hadn't made it into the doghouse yet.* It seemed that Brice had cut most everyone out of his life. *Why? What made you change so much, Brice?* Something major had to have gone down. All this time she had thought it was only her, and he had somehow grown tired of their relationship. In taking this job, she realized there was much more going on with him than she knew. Maybe over the next few weeks the answers to her many questions would be revealed. Although, she wasn't sure she wanted to know.

Her heart had been broken with his cold dismissal, and it had taken time to stow the aching pain associated with the memories of Brice Henderson. *Better I think of him as an asshole than not.* After all, he hadn't tried to get in contact with her again. *No, keep your distance, Lena, and guard your heart. What's done is done.*

ONE OF THE things he hated most about winter was the damn cold morning runs. The last few years he'd run religiously no matter what the weather. This morning was far too cold even for him. *One day won't throw off anything.* It wasn't only for the physical activity; it helped burn off any lingering frustrations and kept him clear-headed throughout the day. The lack of a run wasn't going to have an effect on him as much as it was on his staff. If they were smart, and they usually were, they would quickly pick up on the signals and wouldn't push their luck today.

He usually rushed to shower, dress, and go to his lab, but no one was going to be in until nine, so he had plenty of time to catch up on the world news. *It would be nice to have my coffee now.*

Lena had been able to handle the calls and his every demand just as Nancy had promised. She hadn't made one mistake. Brice hated to admit it, but he was impressed with how she'd handled her first week. Not that he'd spent any time with her, but his staff had no problem reporting back. They were extremely loyal and seemed to have the motto: he who finks first finks best. *As long as they are only giving me the intel and not sharing mine, I don't care what they do.*

When he and Lena had been dating, he'd never doubted her capability and responsibility, but she hadn't seemed quite as focused or driven back then as she was now. Something had changed. Lena was more confident and outspoken than before. *Damn it. I've gone on with life after her, and have tried to put her out of my mind. Singularly focused on my career. But seeing her again now? It's as though no time has passed. She's intelligent, perceptive, and even more beautiful than before. She's even sexier. Fuck.*

Brice never second-guessed his decisions. Even now he knew the choice to end their relationship three years ago was the correct one. Lena wanted something he wasn't ready for then or now. The look in her eyes that night had said it all. *She was falling in love with me.* It was a split-second decision that he'd made that night, but it was the kindest thing he could've done. End it quickly.

He'd known he'd hurt her; the expression on her face had been one of utter shock. But he'd made a decision that had flipped his entire life on its axis, and even though he'd cared about her, he couldn't have taken the next step if he were worrying about how his choices affected anyone else's life. *It had been all about me.*

He had recently left his father's company and had needed to focus on getting his own business off the ground. It hadn't been something that had happened overnight. In fact, had it not been for bumping into his old friend, Asher Barrington, it probably wouldn't have been as close to going live then as it was today. Yes, he had the chemical engineering background, and the formula was all his. But Asher brought something to the team he didn't care about, then or now.

He handled everything in Trundaie, from building the plant to getting all the governmental paperwork, or whatever he called it, taken care of in that country.

Though he wasn't his father, he wasn't sure how far the apple had fallen from that tree. Growing up in a house without a mother figure was difficult, but the revolving door of nannies over the years was more than any of his siblings could take. When the nanny became close to them in any way, she was gone the next day. Six kids were raised by a father who treated women without respect. At least none he'd ever seen. As he thought back to the few women he had seen his father with late at night, they looked more like hookers picked up from a street corner than actual dates. *Maybe they were.* His father abruptly stopped bringing them to the house when Brice became old enough to question who they were.

He always wondered why a man with so much wealth couldn't find a woman to love him. *Maybe he was just as abusive to them as he was to us.* Brice remembered the last day his father ever hit him. He hadn't returned on time after one of his late night football games. Instead of going right home, he'd decided to have some fun with one of the cheerleaders. He was hours past his curfew, but he thought if he was careful and quiet, he would be able to slip into the house unnoticed. That hadn't been the case. For some unknown reason, his father decided to wait up for him. *Why had he that night?* When the smeared lipstick was seen on his cheek, he gave Brice a backhanded slap across the face. Brice wasn't sure what possessed him to do it, but he grabbed his father and jacked him up against that wall. "Touch me again and it will be the last thing you ever do."

His father never laid another hand on him, though he wasn't so sure about his siblings. He was too young at that time to take the weight of responsibility for them all on his shoulders. By the time he was out of college, he was the liaison for all family issues that arose between his siblings and their father. Most were still in college, and he made sure they had an apartment of their own instead of moving back home after they graduated. Of course, he'd only accomplished that by working for his father at Poly-Shyn. The day he walked out of that company, they must have felt as though he walked out on them.

That's the furthest thing from the truth. I did this for all of us. He knew someone needed to break away, make a secure, new path for them all. He had hoped they would want to one day join him in running this new company. Unfortunately, they were no more interested in working for him than they were in working for their father. *Who could blame them? We are both assholes.*

Brice hadn't realized how much time had passed. *And people wonder why I don't like quiet time.* Still with his towel wrapped around his waist, he walked over to the closet on the far wall. He pulled out a clean pair of boxers and removed the towel, throwing it off to the side.

That was when he heard the sound of something breaking on the floor behind him. Spinning around, he saw Lena with what used to be his coffee, now mixed with the remnants of a ceramic mug on the floor. As he gave her a full-frontal, her mouth was wide open. *It's not like you haven't seen it before.*

Though she appeared shocked, Brice noticed her eyes roaming up and down, taking in all of him before she turned away, flushed, and scurried from the room. His body filled with want for her. *I need her or a cold shower.* With his boxers in hand, he walked to the office door he had left open earlier and slammed it closed. *Damn, I want her.*

Chapter Five

P URE MUSCLE. LENA had to force herself to look away, but only after taking in every sweet, sexy inch of him. The only thing that had changed over the years was how more defined and cut he was, if that was even possible. *This man doesn't need Photoshop.* How she wanted to run her hand over his broad shoulders and biceps to his chiseled pecs and rock-hard abs. And when her eyes roamed even lower, her pulse raced as she yearned for what once was. Though it seemed an eternity, only a brief second had passed, yet she saw him growing hard before her eyes. *God, you're perfect.* Instantly she felt a familiar heat growing within her. It had been so long since she'd felt his lips and hands caressing her and making her beg for more as he entered her deeply. *God, I want him. Would one touch be so bad?* That was a stupid question, one she didn't need to answer. *Pull yourself together. There's no room in your life for that.* Walking out of his office, she ignored the broken cup and coffee on the floor. She would call housekeeping because there was no way she was returning to his office to clean the mess until he was back in the lab.

As she sat at her desk, she could hear her heart pounding in her chest. All week she'd successfully avoided speaking to him. *Mostly because he never acknowledges my presence.* Although she had wished for a bit more interaction, seeing him naked was far beyond her expectations. *You never put this on the list, Nancy.* That was a lot more than a person in a temp position could have imagined. *What the hell was he doing running around naked with the door open in the first place?* Her cheeks flushed from want and turned to anger. Had he planned this? Did he want her to see him? Was he thinking he was so damn hot she wouldn't be able to resist him and would go running into his arms, begging him to make love to her? He was wrong. *It's tempting, very tempting, but I'm not going to be your play toy, Brice. You made it clear I wasn't what you wanted then, and I don't want you now.*

Even as she thought the words, her body defied her. *How could I still be so attracted to him when he hurt me as callously as he did?* Thankfully she'd had the strength not to let a moment of lust take control of her, and she'd been able to walk away. *Barely. If he had been closer, had touched me or kissed me, I would have been lost. Damn you, Brice.* I am no child and far from an innocent. Being sexually attracted to a man was a normal healthy response. *Just not this man.*

It was too late. Her initial fears when she saw Brice was her boss had come true. No matter how little they saw each other, the chemistry, when they were close to each other, was still there. *At least for me.* He had been right when he'd said no, he wasn't doing this. Why had she been so confident that she could? *Because I thought I was long over him.* She was mistaken. Something within her didn't hate him as much as she pretended. *Do I quit now? What will that accomplish? I need the money for Nicholas and me.* There wasn't an easy answer or at least not one that didn't have consequences. No, quitting wasn't going to resolve anything. It was too late; she'd already seen him naked. What worse could happen? There was no way she would ever get involved with him intimately again so leaving now would only hurt her financially. *I'm a grown woman. I can handle this.*

Pushing her chair from her desk, she went to make Brice another cup of coffee. This time, she didn't take it to him to leave it on his desk. She placed it on the corner of hers with hopes he would grab it on his way to the lab. Maybe she would get lucky, and he would be running rushing to get to the lab like every other day and not stop to greet her. Never would she have wished to be ignored before.

Lena turned on her computer, and then it hit her. *Well, that didn't go as planned. So much for trying to impress him and come in a few minutes early. That's never happening again. Everything here is only temporary.*

IT MAY BE bitching cold outside, but fuck, it is hotter than hell in here. It was going to take a lot more than a cool shower to remove the need to bury himself deep inside her. *You don't have time for this shit right now.* Brice finished buttoning his shirt and slipped on his jacket. He knew he should talk to her about what happened earlier, but that was a conversation he wanted to have outside the office. A place where they could express themselves any way they chose. *I'd much rather show her, than tell her anyway.*

He expected to see her at her desk when he left his office. Unfortunately, there was only a new cup of coffee. It wasn't like her not to be there. Maybe she was avoiding him. *That might be the wisest choice for both of us.*

Grabbing the cup, he headed to the lab. It was the one place where he couldn't afford or accept any distractions.

Once the doors opened and he sat down at the computer, he was all business. It was like flipping a switch and shutting off the rest of the world, something not many people could do. Whether that was a positive thing or not, it worked for him with the type of work he was doing. Lack of concentration could end in serious injury or worse, death. And not just for him. He may be testing this compound in small amounts, but that didn't mean it wasn't equally dangerous. Every member of his team understood the risk and knew if there was a day they couldn't function at one hundred ten percent, they shouldn't show up for work because he wasn't taking anything less than that. *Surround yourself with the best and demand nothing less from them.* It was a motto he used in all aspects of his life. *The apple didn't fall far from the tree.*

The workday was half over when the phone rang. A rare occurrence. "What is it?"

"Mr. Henderson, your sister is on the line," Lena said.

Why so formal? He didn't need an answer to that question. Brice couldn't be distracted from his goal, and her cold attitude toward him was only making that easier. "Tell her I'll call her tonight."

"She said it's important."

Great, what did Dad do now? Since she never called until it was urgent, he hated to put her off any longer. It was almost lunchtime, so he'd take the call. "Put her through."

"Brice, thanks for taking my call," Zoey said.

"Lena said it's urgent. What's going on?"

There was a long pause before she spoke. "It's Dad."

He had expected that. His father never treated Zoey very nicely. When he did speak to her, she probably wished he hadn't. "What did he do now?"

"He's in the hospital. He had a heart attack."

Dad. They weren't close at all. Hadn't even spoken one word since he walked away from the family business. If he had thought calling him would have changed anything he would have, but his father was the most stubborn man he knew. No heart attack was going to take him down, at least not for long. "Thanks for letting me know."

"Brice, it's not good. The doctors say he is really weak. I'm not sure he's going to make it." Her voice broke as she spoke the last few words.

It had been a long time since he'd had to comfort his baby sister. Usually, it was because she was angry at their father, and rightfully so. Hearing her emotional and filled with worry was a first for him. *I don't get it. He's such an ass and made our lives hell every chance he got.* His sister might be all teary-eyed over his father's suffering, but he wasn't. The man would be back on his feet and raising hell faster than you could count to one hundred.

"Did you hear me, Brice? It's really serious."

"Zoey, he'll be all right. I have work to finish." *Not that I'm going to get anything done after this call.*

He could hear her sniffling over the line. "He wants to see you."

Now that I don't believe. "Zoey, I get it. You always try to fix everything. Some things can't be fixed."

"This is not my request; it was his. I know your history and God knows you know mine. But something is different about him right now. I'm not sure if it's because he is so sick, or if it's the medicine, but I'm telling you, he asked for you specifically. And it wasn't a demand, more like he was pleading for me to make sure I got you here." The line went quiet for a minute before she continued, her voice now soft and pleading. "If you can't do it for him, please, do it for me. Come to the hospital and see him before it's too late."

As far as Brice was concerned it already was too late.

What could his father have to say that he would want to hear? *Sorry isn't going to cut it. Not after all this time.* At least not for him.

Zoey had never asked for anything before. Why did she have to go so big with her first request? He had promised her that he'd always be there when she needed him. *Does this qualify as one of those times?* "I'll think about it."

"I know you'll do the right thing, Brice."

Really? My track record doesn't reflect that. He hung up the phone and buzzed Lena's desk.

"Yes, Mr. Henderson."

Every time she called him that, it made him want to pull her into his arms and kiss her passionately until she cried out his name again and again. "Hold all my calls for the remainder of the day. I'll be heading out. You can reach me on my cell phone if anything urgent comes up."

"Yes, Mr.—"

Brice hung up the phone before she could finish. *First I see my father. Then Lena, you and I have some unfinished business and there is nothing I would enjoy more than having you in my bed, but not before this project is completed.* Everything he wanted was within his grasp. *Stay focused Brice. It's what I demand from my staff. I lead by example. Work comes above all.*

Chapter Six

BRICE ENTERED THE ICU and headed right for the nurses station. "I'm here to see James Henderson, my father." The last two words were spoken much softer. He was neither proud nor embarrassed about him. It felt more like indifference, and that seemed so much worse.

"Mr. Henderson is in room eight. He is still weak and heavily medicated. The doctors request visits to be short so he can rest."

When he walked into the hospital room he was taken aback by what he saw. It wasn't the first time he had been in a hospital room but never for a family member. The only sounds were the light beeping of heart monitors not only in his room but throughout the unit.

His father appeared to be sleeping, so he sat in the only chair in the room. From his seat, he had a clear view of his father's face. It had been more than three years since they'd seen each other, and time hadn't been kind to his father. *You look twenty years older, Dad. Guess you haven't changed your ways, have you?*

His father looked gray. Brice had never pictured his

father weak. In any way. The man had been the most formidable businessman he'd ever come across. That made leaving Poly-Shyn and starting B&H Advanced Engineering with Asher Barrington all the riskier. His father might not have the chemical engineering background that he did, but he was one ruthless man who didn't care what it took to get the job done. Results were all that mattered, and if it meant crushing his son's company to achieve them, he would do it and never look back.

Either his father didn't see B&H as a viable threat or he hadn't bothered following what his flesh and blood was building and becoming. *Both a mistake on your part, Dad. I'm your biggest threat and always have been.*

Brice was no longer a child who needed to be coddled. There were many nights as a young boy when he'd wished to have someone there to tell him it was only a bad dream, that everything was going to be okay. How any father could have children and not be there for them, in good times or bad, was beyond him.

Sitting in the room with nothing but his thoughts wasn't a place he wanted to be for long. Bringing up the past would only hinder the outcome he strived for in his future. Getting up from the cold plastic chair, he walked to the side of the bed. *Guess you weren't the one who wanted me here, Dad.* His voice full of sarcasm, he said gruffly, "Yeah, this has been a great talk; let's do this again in another three years." *Good try, Zoey.*

When he turned to walk out, he saw his youngest

brother Dean standing in the doorway. His hair was wild, as though he just gotten out of bed. *Knowing you, Dean, you probably did.*

"Good ole Dad asked to see you too?"

Dean shook his head. "Dad had only one child he cared anything about, Brice, and that's you."

It wasn't jealousy in his brother's voice. Over the years, they all learned very fast if Dad noticed you in any way, you would only experience his wrath. Your only hope each day was to go unnoticed. Brice was the most vocal back then and probably still was today.

"Zoey called you too, I take it?"

Nodding, Dean replied, "Yeah, said you were going to be here. That I might want to come and make sure you were okay."

Arching a brow, Brice asked, "Did you think you would find me sitting here all emotional?"

Laughing, Dean said, "Hell, no. More worried you were going to get caught doing something stupid like pulling the plug."

Don't think that didn't cross my mind. "I'm not quite that bad. At least not today."

"Since Zoey was able to pry you away from your lab, want to go to the pub and grab a beer?"

"Not today, Dean, but soon. There is something that still needs my attention at my lab." *My lab? Fuck it. After a day like today, I'm not accomplishing shit in there. But there's something at the office that can't wait any longer.*

LENA FOUND HERSELF totally relaxed the entire time Brice was out of the office, not needing to be prepared for him to round the corner and get her pulse racing. *It should be like this every day.* For the first time since she started the job earlier that week, she was able to concentrate solely on the task at hand. *Amazing what I can do when you're not here.*

There was only an hour left until finishing time. As she sat typing, completing the final daily entries, she sensed someone watching her. Spinning in her office chair she found Brice standing there, watching her, not saying a word. "Bri . . . Mr. Henderson, I thought you weren't returning to the office today."

"Plans changed." He didn't move past her to his office. Instead, he stood still watching her.

She wanted to say something sarcastic, but there was a look in his eyes that she hadn't seen before. Lena couldn't pinpoint it. It didn't look like sadness, but something close. Had something happened with Zoey? She was the call he received before leaving so abruptly. Whatever it was, she could see it was troubling him. "Why don't you go to your office, and I'll bring you some coffee." *Even that is more than I should be doing. Don't ask anything personal. That door slammed shut long ago, and don't you open it again, Lena.*

Brice nodded and did as she suggested. Only when she found herself alone again did she realize how tense she had become. Every nerve was on edge. *Damn you, Brice. I don't want to want you.* Pushing away from her desk, she rose and went to get his coffee. *Why did I offer?* She knew why. It was because no matter how much she said otherwise, she still cared about him. He had been after all, a man she'd loved very much. Was it wrong for her to be kind to him now? *Wrong, no. Stupid, most definitely.* It was too late to take back the words now. He was probably sitting there wondering what was taking her so long. Making his coffee, one cream and two sugars, like he always had it, she headed for his office.

Go in, put it down, and get out. Don't look at him. That little pep talk she gave herself flew out the window when she saw him half-sitting on the edge of his desk, facing her and holding a glass of what looked like bourbon in his hand. Lena had never seen him drink during the day before. Whatever was troubling him earlier was still on his mind.

"Is everything okay?" She hadn't meant to let the question leave her lips. He didn't answer, only continued to stare at her for another moment before downing his drink. His eyes softened to almost a crystal blue. When she looked into them it was as if she were looking into the ocean, causing waves of emotion to come crashing within her. Lena walked over and handed him his coffee. "Try this."

Brice reached out and took it from her, setting the coffee mug on his desk. "That's not going to cut it today."

She searched his eyes for answers but found none. As if she hadn't made enough mistakes already, Lena stepped closer and touched his left shoulder tenderly, trying to offer some form of comfort.

Brice reacted, grabbing her wrist fiercely and pulling her up against him. His nostrils flared, and his eyes darkened as they met hers. Lena opened her mouth to protest, but she instantly forgot what she was going to say as his mouth captured hers. His mouth was hot and tasted of bourbon as his tongue traced hers. *Stop; don't do this. I can't.* She pleaded internally for it to end, yet her body was reacting to him with a need almost greater than his.

Their tongues were in an intimate dance as she clung to him. Her body quivered when he slid his arms around her, pulling her even closer. Her breasts, now pressed hard against his, ached to be released from their confines.

With one strong move, he lifted her into his arms and carried her to stand by the leather couch, his lips never leaving hers. *Lena, what are you doing? You don't want this. It's not too late. Stop it now.*

His hand came up, cupping her breast and pinching her taut nipple through the delicate fabric. Lena pulled her lips away from his, arching back, moaning in pleasure. *Why are you doing this to me? Why?* His hand moved to the other breast to give equal attention, as his mouth nipped at her neck and collarbone then trailed up the other side. Against her ear he whispered, "Tell me you want me," he bit her earlobe gently, "that you need this as much as I do."

Brice removed his hold on her only long enough to

rip open his shirt, and toss it to one side. Once her hands touched his bare chest, she knew she was lost. The heat in the pit of her stomach was growing faster than she could think. It had been so long since she had felt his touch. No matter how wrong this was, if she stopped now, the pain was going to be unbearable.

"I need to see all of you, Lena." Brice's voice was husky with desire. He unbuttoned her shirt, then moved his hands so they slid under the fabric and slipped it off her shoulders, letting it drop to the floor. Her bare flesh heated at his touch.

With one hand she reached behind her, unhooked her white lace bra, and let it fall to the floor. Brice growled as he watched her. "God, you're beautiful."

He pulled her back into his arms, kissing her passionately. As he continued exploring her mouth, she felt his hands slide beneath her skirt and raise it to her waist. His hand found the top of a stocking and began to slowly ease it down her thigh.

Lena lifted her leg so he could remove one stocking, then the other. Tingles of excitement flowed through her as his hands trailed up again, this time caressing her bare skin. His hands were strong, and each touch became firmer as their need grew. Finally, they settled on her ass, his fingers digging in as he pulled her against him so she could feel his hard shaft pressed against her abdomen. *God, I need him.*

The pulsing need between her legs begged for his attention. "Please. I need—"

In one quick movement, she felt him tear her white lace panties from her, letting them fall. Brice pulled away slightly, moving his hand to touch her delicate folds. *Please, yes, Brice.* His knee prodded her to open for him. Closing her eyes, she did so. Instantly she felt him slide a finger between her folds and over her clit then back again. Moaning in pleasure she opened her legs wider, needing more of him. He didn't comply. Instead, he slowly traced the path again and again. She wanted to rip his remaining clothes off. She had been so long without the touch of a man. *Not just any man, but you, Brice, your touch. I've missed being cheirshed.*

As she moved her hands lower and tried to unhook his belt, he grabbed both her wrists with one hand and pulled them away.

"When I'm ready."

She was ready now. Was he trying to kill her with these teasing touches? Wiggling her hips, she tried to get him to give her what she wanted, what she needed, but he adjusted his hand. Now his thumb circled her clit, increasing in speed, faster and faster. Then he slowed before starting again. *Sweet torture.*

Lena could feel her heart beating erratically. He continued to bring her to the brink and hold her there. Her legs trembled and threatened to give way. The last time he slowed his pace he slipped a finger deep inside her. He let go of her wrist, wrapped an arm around her waist to support her, and entered her again and again.

"Yeah, baby. That's it. Let go. Give me what I want,"

Brice demanded as he added a second finger.

Not being able to hold back, her body began to shudder with wave after wave as he took her over the edge, her moans of pleasure echoing through the room.

Before her body started to relax, she heard the sound of his buckle and zipper being undone. One moment she was fluttering back to earth from her sexual bliss, the next she found herself being scooped into his arms with her legs wrapped around him. Her wet softness now pressed against his hard, throbbing cock.

"Are you on the pill?" Brice asked.

Her only response was a nod before he filled her with one powerful move. Her body clenched around him, and he gripped her hips and positioned her so he could go deeper. Never breaking rhythm, he thrust again and again, harder and deeper, until each stroke sent waves of pleasure through them both. Cries of ecstasy escaped her lips, muffled only by the sound of his. Their climaxes were all consuming, leaving them shuddering against each other.

As the pulsing eased, Brice kissed her tenderly then set her down, so she once again was standing on the floor.

"Damn, that was as sweet as I remember, and why I never could forget you," Brice said while still holding her.

Coming back to her senses, his words hit home, cutting her to the core. Lena knew this was a mistake even before he spoke. But with everything they had shared in the past, *this* was what he remembers? Had it only been a sexual fulfillment for him back then? *How could I have been so foolish to fall into the same trap? I mean nothing to him but great sex.*

She wasn't about to give him the satisfaction of seeing how hurt she was. In fact, she wasn't even going to acknowledge it was a mind-blowing experience for her. Picking up her clothes from the floor, she began to dress.

Once they were dressed Brice said, "Have dinner with me and spend the night."

If he thought this one-time lapse in judgment was going to get her back in his bed, picking up where they left off, he was out of his flipping mind. Meeting his gaze, she said flatly, "I have plans."

"Break them."

Not for all the gold in the world. "Brice, this was a one-time-only mistake. I don't plan on letting it happen again. I think it's best if we keep our personal life and business life separate."

He reached out for her hand and pulled her up against him. "Say what you want now, Lena, but you felt it, too."

Oh, I did. God, it was wonderful. Amazing. But that changed nothing. Three years she'd worked to forget he even existed. Now her body still tingled from his touch.

She could hear the phone ringing at her desk. Pulling her hand free she said, "If you'll excuse me, I have work to finish."

The room was filled with his laughter as she walked

out of the office. *Damn you, Brice Henderson. Why did I let you do this to me? Again.* Sitting at her desk gathering her things, she realized it wasn't him, it was her. She had wanted him and had practically begged him to make love to her. Why should he think any differently now? *Oh, what have I done?* It had felt so good to be in his arms again, to have him inside her. Even better than she had remembered, and it was fantastic then. *How was that possible?* But the man who'd tossed her aside so easily was the same driven and ambitious man who had just fucked her senseless. *Why had he pursued me? He'd discarded me so easily before. Is that his plan now?* She was angered with herself for allowing this to happen. *I'm worth so much more than that. It will not be repeated. Ever.*

Chapter Seven

THANKFULLY THE BUS ride back home to Plymouth wasn't the normal overcrowded trip for a Friday night. That would've made the already dreaded experience of a weekend in her childhood home all the more difficult.

Home wasn't a horrible place. She loved growing up in a small town. She could ride her bike freely. *As free as one can get with two older brothers watching my every move.* There was one negative about it. In such a small community, everyone knew everything about everyone and news traveled quickly. *Especially bad news.*

She knew, without a doubt, what was about to happen. People who she had not seen since she was pregnant would approach her with forced smiles to tell her what a charming and cute child Nicholas was. He was a cutie, but Lena knew their interest was more than how much he had grown. They were on a fishing expedition, and each one of them wanted to be the one who brought back the biggest catch. *The latest and greatest for the gossip hotline.*

Lena had never cared what others thought or said about her. And over the last few years she'd given them a reason to gossip. Eventually, all the chatter would find its way to her parents. That only increased the odds of her parents getting all riled up on the one subject that caused them to argue each time they saw each other. *Nicholas's father.* She'd never told them his name and why they persisted in asking was beyond her.

It didn't help that they believed the father was someone in Plymouth. Each time she had returned home her mother insisted on talking about men around her age and watching for her reaction, in case she gave away her little secret. Would they ever understand Nicholas was better off without him in his life? *Probably not.*

Nicholas lay sound asleep across her seat, his head on her lap. Lena brushed his dark curls from his forehead. *We should be there soon.* The trip from Boston took only an hour, but with a child who was full of energy when she picked him up from daycare, it seemed much longer. She had tried reading to him, then singing to him, but nothing would quiet him for some reason. He was too young to understand where they were going, so that couldn't be the issue.

Could it be he sensed her anxiety from her encounter with Brice? She had tried to shake it off before picking him up. She tried telling herself it meant nothing, only a temporary lapse in judgment, but that wasn't the truth. When he'd opened the door that very first day and their eyes had met, she'd known she was lost. No matter how hard she tried to tell herself she was over him, hated him, it was far from the truth. Brice was her first and only love. *Unfortunately, I was not his.*

The bus driver announced their arrival over the microphone. Nicholas was so exhausted he didn't even flinch. *Poor baby. It's been a rough week for you too, hasn't it?* Pulling him into her arms, she wrapped him in the blanket and departed. Her oldest brother Jason was waiting there to meet them.

He grabbed her bags from her hands and said, "The folks are still out shopping. I don't know what is up, but Mom had Dad clear out my old room." He turned and looked at Lena. "Are you moving back or something?"

God no. Her heart pounded in her chest. She hoped her parents weren't planning on her staying. She agreed to a weekend. No more. Living in their house would mean living by their rules. She wasn't great at following them when she was younger, and that hadn't improved with age. "Jason, I'm thirty years old and have a child. Do you think I would survive a week, never mind a month, living here?" She didn't wait for him to answer. His expression said it all. Jason had been the first to leave the house right after college. He may still live locally, but not *with* them.

"So what do you think they're planning then?"

Lena buckled Nicholas in the car seat in the back and hopped in beside him. "Your guess is as good as mine. You know Mom. When she sets her mind fixed on something, she won't stop until she gets her way. Maybe she is going to finally make that sewing room she has been talking about for years. Dad always hated having all her supplies all over the dining room table on Tuesday nights when her quilting buddies came over." *Please let it be that. I don't need more pressure than I have already.*

Jason nodded. "You could be right."

By his tone she knew he didn't buy that either. Her mother was up to something and, unfortunately, it had to do with her and Nicholas. Looks like this is going to be a long weekend. *Why did I agree to come?*

EVERYONE HAD GONE home, and the lab was quiet. Exactly how he liked to work. The formula was testing positive on all counts. Things really couldn't be looking any better at this point. He hadn't heard from Asher all week, and he took that as a good sign. Normally when he called it was to confirm everything was still on target. Brice wasn't someone who needed to be monitored. It pissed him off each time Asher called and questioned him on the status. "You handle your end of the business and let me worry about mine," Brice had said. *Guess he got the message.*

With all the distractions today he thought he wouldn't be able to accomplish shit, but surprisingly he was able to get several uninterrupted hours of data into the computer. *God knows I needed them.* His staff was reliable, yet when under pressure, they became jumpy. When he'd walked over to speak to one of the chemists earlier, he had been so nervous he'd almost dropped the laptop he was carrying. Brice knew he had become more demanding as time went on, but everyone knew that before they signed up for this job. *I don't pretend to be anything I'm not.* He was, after all, his father's son.

Leaning back in his chair, he let his mind wander, thinking how his father had looked lying in that hospital bed. Was Zoey right? Was his father so ill he wasn't going to pull through? He had wanted to ask the doctors his status, but couldn't bring himself to do it. No matter how bad things were between them, that was his father, and he should care. *Then why don't I?*

Brice didn't deny things were bad between them, but over the last few years he'd rarely thought about it. It was the choice he had made: to put all of that in the past and only look toward his future. It seemed like only yesterday they had their blow-out fight, and he'd walked out of his father's office. *How had three years gone by so quickly?* His father looked like he'd aged twenty years, and he couldn't remember the last time he had seen his youngest brother, Dean, never mind his other three brothers. The only one he kept in contact with was Zoey. *And that was because she wouldn't stop until I took her call.*

He was sure they understood; they had grown up in that same household. Each and every one of them had physical or emotional scars from the abuse. Some of them more than others. How they were allowed to stay with their father was beyond him. Maybe being one of the richest men on the East Coast gave him the connections to pay off the right people to stay away and shut up. *Money covered a multitude of sins, and with Dad, I'm surprised he didn't dole out every cent he had.* Whatever it was that kept them all together living in that house, their family had been anything but a happy one. *Never was and never would be a happy family.*

That cold thought wasn't something Zoey would ever admit. No, she pushed him to always look on the bright side of things. To forgive and forget. That might work for her, but it would never work for him. Brice's scars weren't visible, but the emotional ones ran deep, always worried he was more like his father than his siblings. For his entire life he had distanced himself from everyone. Never allowing anyone to get close. *Anyone except Lena.*

There had been so many women before her, and he'd never looked at them with any serious intentions. He called on them only to occupy his nights then moved on. But from the moment Lena spilled her iced coffee down the front of his dress shirt, he'd been lost. Her dark eyes filled with embarrassment as she unsuccessfully tried to wipe it off. "I would take off mine and give it to you, but your chest is so broad, mine won't fit." Brice had been tempted to take her offer of her shirt right then, but he had sensed she was not as experienced as he was at that time. *But she had been a fast learner.*

In a matter of weeks she had been able to penetrate the fortress he had built around himself. It was a time when he thought he had everything. A great job working for his father at Poly-Shyn and a hot and sexy young woman on his arm. But she was so much more than that. When he was with her, he felt like a different person. Yes, they had the most amazing sex he had ever experienced, but that was only one piece of their relationship. It had been a time when he relaxed, slowed down, spent quiet evenings doing nothing but enjoying her company.

That's when I had the time to spare. There is no room for such things now. If he hadn't broken things off with her then, he wouldn't be where he was today. Success came with sacrifices. Sacrifices he still intended to make. He wouldn't allow everything he had worked hard for slip through his fingers. Yes, he'd had wanted her and felt sated for taking her. *It still was the best sex of his life.*

The last thing he needed was the responsibility to care for another person. He was free to come and go as he pleased. No one hounding him about why he didn't come home after work. He ate what he wanted, when he wanted, and did only things that pleased him. *If anyone has an issue with that, it's their fucking problem. Not mine.*

What would please him right now would be having Lena again. Closing his eyes, he could almost feel how silky soft she'd felt against him. Her body had always enticed him, but something was different. Her hips were rounder than he recalled, and her ass curved perfectly as he cupped it in his hands. *The one thing that hasn't changed is how damn responsive she is when I touch her.*

He could feel his cock harden with need. Brice wanted her in his arms again, not later, but now. *Damn, why didn't you take me up on my offer?* She said she had plans.

After their hot little afternoon fuck, what could she possibly have found more enticing than going another round? She had said it was a one-time thing, but that was not what he wanted. He recalled a time when they'd spent an entire day in bed enjoying what each other had to offer. Had she forgotten?

He knew there was no way she was spending the weekend alone. But who was she with? If it was a boyfriend, he didn't mean all that much to her, not the way she'd melted in his arms.

When he thought of some other man having her right now, it pulled at the pit of his stomach. Getting up from his desk, he pushed his chair back and walked out of the lab. *Damn you, Lena. I closed that door years ago. I'm not going to open it again.* He wouldn't care. She meant nothing to him. They were purely two people who needed their sexual needs released. Nothing more.

Chapter Eight

"NANA. NANA." LENA heard Nicholas shouting from the other room. It was a bittersweet sound. How she wished her son could have more family surrounding him, but the closer they became, the harder it was living in Boston.

Her father came to sit by her on the couch. "Your mother is having one heck of a time getting little Nicky to eat his vegetables. If I remember right, you were a picky eater at that age too."

Lena turned to face him. "I'll eat almost anything."

Her father laughed. "Not at two. I remember some little girl taking her peas and flicking them one by one onto the floor. Of course our collie didn't mind that so much."

I love peas. Some things do change over time. And by the sounds of her mother's voice in the other room, having a grandchild in the house changed a lot.

"Maybe I should go and check on them."

When she started to get up, her father took her hand and stopped her. "Lena, give them some time alone. It will be fine. Your mother was able to raise three children; I'm sure she can sweet talk this one just like she did you guys."

He was probably right. Her mother had a way of saying just the right thing, and without even knowing it, Lena found herself doing what she said she was not in any way going to do, under any circumstances. Nicholas's high-pitched laughter echoed through the house. *Looks like you haven't lost your touch, Mom.*

Sitting back again, now more relaxed, she turned to her father again. "I'm glad we came this weekend. Nicholas is enjoying it."

"We love having him here and you, too. It has been too long." Before she could stop him he went right down the guilt-trip path she had avoided the past two days. "I know things were difficult between you and your mother at first, but you have to forgive her for what she said. She may not have handled it correctly, but neither did you." He patted her hand as he spoke. "You might think you are doing the right thing now, but a boy needs a man around to show him certain things."

Like how to leave the toilet seat up? No, thank you. "Dad, I . . . we . . . are doing fine. I can do this. Many women raise children alone now. Having a father is a plus but no longer a requirement."

His face looked shocked. "So having me in your life wasn't all that important to you?"

Oh shit. Will I ever learn not to put my foot in my mouth? Wrapping her arms around her father, she said not only the words he needed to hear but the ones that reflected what was in her heart. "Dad, you are, and always have been, the most important man in my life."

He hugged her gently then pulled away to look into her eyes. "I know, pumpkin. But I am talking about Nicholas. I remember taking you and your brothers out deep-sea fishing early in the morning while your mother stayed home, baking cookies for your school parties. We would spend hours out there. Do you think it was all about fishing for me?"

Lena sat there quietly. She hadn't given it much thought. Those were special times they'd spent together, but until he mentioned it, she had thought of it as him with his boys and having to take the one girl with them to ruin it. She always had felt in the way. *Was I wrong?*

"It was because I wanted to spend time with you. To watch your eyes light up when you recalled your big catch of the day was better than any fishing trips with my buddies. You might not be ready for him to be in Nicholas's life right now, but don't close that door for good. Things change, people change. He might not be ready now to be a father, but if he chooses to one day, don't shut him out in revenge for his actions from the past. It will only be Nicholas who suffers later."

Was it getting easier to hear the same lecture or had the message changed over the years? She had to admit, this one pulled at her heartstrings, where the other times she only got pissed off.

"Lena, one of these days, you are going to find yourself a fine young man who is going to take my place." When Lena opened her mouth to correct him, he put his finger up and stopped her. "Whoever this man is who hurt you like he did, you have to let it go. If you don't you will never have room in that big heart of yours for Mr. Right. He's out there waiting for you. You just have to let him in." Her father let out a soft chuckle. "Besides, I have a wedding fund set aside for you, and if you don't use it, I might have to take a trip around the world with your mother, and you know how much I hate to fly."

He and Mom weren't only a team, but their lives had been much richer because of their sacrifices. Lena knew her father would never use that money for a trip around the world. It had always been family first. *Is he right? Is refusing to let go of my anger with Brice holding me back, not allowing me to move forward?*

Her focus had only been on her son. Yes, she was lonely, but dating again scared the hell out of her. Lena had thought about joining a love-match site and had done searches on them a few times. It wasn't for her. Not that she didn't believe people could find love there, she had already found love once and still hadn't recovered fully from the loss. *Sorry, Dad, but marriage isn't in my future.*

Lena understood her father's fear. He was worried there was no one to take care of his baby girl. *Sometimes it scares me too.* It was hard, damn hard at times. This wasn't a college course that if you fail you could always take again. She had one shot to make this right: Nicholas. And nothing was going to get in the way of her being the best mother she could be.

No matter how you planned it, life didn't always turn out the way you pictured. Lena, like every young girl, had dreamed of having a glamorous movie star wedding and living in a mansion with her handsome husband who adored her and their children, of course. *At least one dream came true.* She could live without the others.

Look at me now, sitting on the couch on a Saturday night, watching my son run the same circles from kitchen to living room as I did with my brothers. It's a shame you don't have siblings to play with, Nicholas.

Panic filled her for a moment. *At least you better not have one.* She laid a hand on her flat abdomen. *There's no way.* Her heart raced as she thought of how reckless she had been the other afternoon with Brice. How foolish could she have been, letting her desires take control and block out any sense of reality and responsibility? If anyone understood what ninety-nine point nine percent accuracy meant, it was her. Lena had been using birth control pills the first time she became pregnant. The doctor told her it was rare, but it could happen. *What are the odds that can happen twice? Shit.*

"Are you okay, Lena? You look pale."

The concern in her father's voice brought her back to the moment. "I haven't been sleeping well. You remember those nights you stayed up with us when we were teething? Well, it's my turn now." It was true, lack of sleep was affecting her, but that was something she had learned to live with.

"Your mother and I can put Nicholas to bed. Why don't you take advantage of a night off? Go out with your friends. It will do you good."

Going to bed was more in line with what she wanted to do, but maybe he was right. If she got out, got some fresh air, she would feel better about a lot of things. "Are you sure?"

"Nothing would make your mother happier than being able to watch Nicholas a bit longer. Now go before he notices you're gone." He pulled the keys to their Subaru out and handed them to her.

"He isn't used to me not being here when he goes to bed. Nicholas might fuss and not sleep."

"Good thing we've had a lot of practice over the years. Lena, quit making excuses. You know your mother and I can handle anything, and if needed, we'll call you. Now go."

It was her own insecurities that were troubling her. She wasn't leaving him with a stranger. What child doesn't love to have a sleepover with their grandparents? She knew she had when she was little. *Up late and got away with more there than at home.* Maybe it was time to release some of the hold. Besides, he was in the best care anyone could ever ask for.

Leaning over, she gave her father a kiss on the cheek, grabbed her coat from the hallway closet, and headed out. Exactly where to she wasn't sure.

She spent the next half hour driving around in circles. She may have grown up here, but she hadn't lived here for five years. So much had changed in that short period of time. What was happening to her small town? The little mom-and-pop shops were now filled with the same stores you found in the city. Like herself, things moved forward, but it was sad all the same.

Then she came across her favorite after-school hangout. Zips Diner was the one place that stayed open late, and she had gone there many times on a date after a movie. *Oh, those were the days when my biggest worry was being home before my ten o'clock curfew.*

She pulled up, and to her amazement, it was open. *But do you still have the best coffee in town?*

As she entered the diner it hit her: nothing had changed. It was set up exactly as it had been years ago. The inside had the original red leather seats in the booths and at the counter. She used to sit, spinning on those stools while having an ice cream soda after school with her brothers before going home for dinner. They thought back then they were pulling one over on their parents, but now she realized her parents weren't as ignorant about what they were up to as they pretended to be.

Grabbing the booth farthest from the door, she picked up a menu. *Breakfast served all day.* Scanning, she found her favorite: farm fresh eggs with a side of corned beef hash.

The waitress came and took her order then walked away. Such a change from Boston where everyone was always in a rush, running from one place to another. Even the waitress here worked at her own peaceful pace. *I'm so jealous. I can't remember the last time I wasn't watching a clock, having a deadline to meet, or running late for an appointment.*

Her father was right; she needed to get out. If she wasn't at work, she was with her son. Lena couldn't remember the last time she had been alone. *Of course the city doesn't allow for much of that anyway.* Digging in her purse, she pulled out a quarter and placed it in the slot on the tabletop jukebox. *These still can't be here, can they?* The coin clanked as it entered and the light went on. Pressing B2, "Falling in Love with You" began to play. It wasn't a song from her generation, but it was one that meant so much to her parents. Her father still bragged about how he won her mother's heart by singing this song to her back in college.

It wasn't the waitress who delivered her food. It was Rex, her high school sweetheart. The last twelve years had been good to him. *Still as handsome as ever.* "Hi Rex. How are you?"

He sat in the seat across from her. "Hey, Lena. I'm good. Are you just visiting or moving back to town?"

There were many times she'd thought about it. How raising Nicholas would be so different here. He would be able to ride his bike to school and play in the neighborhood park. No subways, no buses, because neither were needed here. But her dreams were filled with so much more. She wanted to work for the biggest and strongest companies there were. Lena finally landed a job, and even though it was temporary, it was one that was about to open doors for her. A company like B&H carried a lot of clout not only in Boston but worldwide. A recommendation from them was exactly what she needed and what she had been striving for. Coming back here would be giving up on everything she'd worked so hard for and would close the door on any future opportunities. Every sacrifice would've been for nothing.

"I'm only here for the weekend to visit the folks." She looked around and noticed there were a few customers. "Are you sure you won't get in trouble for sitting around? I mean there are customers and old man Zip won't be too happy if he catches you."

Rex let out a deep laugh. "Yeah, I've had my share of getting my ass chewed out by him over the years. That's why I bought the place last year. Now I can sit when I want."

He owns this place? Why? "Wow. Guess things have changed. So Rex, why buy this place? I mean, why not open up one of those fancy restaurants? My mother told me you had all the culinary skills needed, so why stay here?"

Rex reached across the table and stole a piece of her toast. "You're telling me that being in Boston is making you happy?"

Sometimes. "It's nice there. So many more opportunities."

He shook his head. "That's not what I asked you. I

have been to Boston, New York, and many cities around the world. A place doesn't make you happy, Lena. Who you are with there does."

He was right. She was in Boston, chasing a career, but not happy. She had blamed it on so many things, but the truth was she hadn't been happy there since Brice dumped her. *So why stay? He'd made it clear he had wanted nothing to do with her.* It was a combination of things. Hoping someday he would come back, begging her forgiveness, and not wanting to have to admit failure and go back home. Was she making a mistake? Obviously Brice was never going to beg for anything and "I'm sorry" probably wasn't in his vocabulary either. Maybe it was time to make another change. There had been so many over the past few years; maybe coming home this weekend was a sign that it was time for another one.

"How is Nicholas doing? That's his name, right?"

He knows my son's name. What else does he know? Smiling, Lena answered, "He's great. My parents are watching him tonight. Dad thought I needed to get out for a while." It felt good to be able to speak about her son and not hide his existence.

"I agree. You need out, away from all that noise. Why don't you finish up and let me take you to a movie?"

Her heart began to pound. *He's asking me out? On a date?* "I can't."

"Why? Do you have a husband or boyfriend who won't be happy about it?"

No one cares what I do. No one at all. "Not that it's any of your business, but no, I do not have either."

"Good, then you have no excuse to say no."

Oh, just as cocky as you were in high school. I hope I'm not going to regret this. "Okay. A movie and that's all."

Lena spent the rest of the evening with Rex. They went to a movie and then out for another cup of coffee. She hadn't laughed so hard in years. They spoke about their school years and what happened to all their friends. Most of them were married with children of their own.

It was after midnight when she finally returned to her parents' house. Closing the door quietly behind her, she made her way to the staircase. Just like when she was a teenager, her father had waited up. "Guess you weren't so tired after all."

Turning around, she felt guilty for staying out so late. "Sorry. I met up with an old friend and time seemed to get away from us."

"So I hear. How is Rex doing by the way? I haven't made it to the diner in a while."

Great. Mother is going to love this. "Good. Did you know he bought the diner?"

"Yes, the whole town celebrated last summer when he signed the papers." Her father arched his brow and said, "We could watch Nicholas again tomorrow if you would like to go out again."

"Dad, we only went out as friends. Nothing more. I'm going back to Boston tomorrow night. I don't want Mom to start thinking I'm moving back home or anything. My job and life are there now." She didn't want her words to sound so ungrateful. It was the furthest from the truth. No one could have asked for better parents. They loved and supported her. It was her stubborn behavior that had put the wedge between them before. She wasn't about to let that happen again. Kissing her father on his forehead, she headed toward the stairs.

"Sweet dreams, pumpkin."

I sure hope so. "Goodnight, Dad."

Once upstairs she checked on Nicholas, who was fast asleep. *Sleep tight, little man.* There was nothing left for her to do but go to bed. Unfortunately sleep didn't come easily. Her mind wandered back to her evening with Rex. It had been nice. Easy. He'd opened doors for her, said all the right things. *God, he was so sweet to me.*

Lying there, she closed her eyes again and could still hear his laughter. She enjoyed being with Rex, so why was she filled with an overwhelming feeling of emptiness? *Dammit.* A few weeks ago this might have been so different. She might have even taken her father's offer and gone out with Rex again. After all these years, he was still single. He'd made it clear he could be interested in starting things again. Had he been thinking of her like she had him when they were in school? *My very first crush.*

Her phone chimed with a message. *Rex.*

"Sweet dreams."

Not sure what to say, she was so confused by every-thing. Trying to figure out one man was bad enough, adding a second in the mix wasn't a good idea. *Since when do I ever do the smart thing?* "Goodnight, Rex."

The timing was off. He was a wonderful guy, but right now, it didn't feel right. There were unresolved issues she had to address back in Boston before she would be totally free to love again.

As she closed her eyes and drifted off to sleep, she had only one person on her mind. Brice. *Thank you for turning back time far enough to screw my life up all over again.*

Thankfully the next day was uneventful. Her mother never mentioned Rex, and more surprisingly, she never even asked about her evening out. Before Lena knew it, they were back on the bus, heading to Boston. Her brother Jason was upset she wouldn't allow him to drive her home, but she insisted they enjoyed the bus ride. The truth was she needed to unwind, to have some time to regroup and gather her thoughts before going to the office tomorrow. If she didn't sort this all out, she knew she would be spending the entire night tossing and turning, and that wasn't going to solve anything.

This ride was different from the last. Nicholas didn't close his eyes once. Instead, he kept saying one word over and over again until she thought she would pull out her hair. "Nana. Nana." *Mom, did you plan this? I wouldn't put it past you.*

Her phone buzzed with a text message. They hadn't been gone fifteen minutes, and she knew it had to be her mother, checking in on them. She was wrong.

"Had a great time last night. Let's do it again soon. Have a safe trip back to Boston. Rex."

She couldn't respond. Part of her wanted to say she'd had a good time as well but another part of her couldn't commit to doing it again. It wasn't fair to either of them right now. Maybe one day, not now. *How can I yearn for someone who doesn't want me, yet have a great guy here who wants to be with me? What a hot mess.* Lena did the only thing she could. She ignored his message.

Finally the network was strong enough on her phone for her to download a cartoon to distract Nicholas. She hated being one of those parents who used an electronic device as a babysitter, but right now anything she could find to distract him was open game. *How do people do it with more than one?* Well, that wasn't something she was going to waste another minute dwelling on. It was just the two of them, and that was fine with her. Her father might think she needed a man in her life, but that wasn't true. She had Nicholas, and they made their own little family. Lena had wanted to tell her father there were things worse than being alone. *Like being with a man who doesn't love you.*

Love wasn't all it was cracked up to be. Look where it got her last time. Broken-hearted and alone. *No thanks.* She wasn't going down that path again. What she needed to do was deny her physical needs. But the way he'd looked at her and made her feel when he'd touched her was like a flame she couldn't resist. Her hand yearned to reach out and touch it, even though she knew she was going to get burned. *Who would be able to resist that?*

She had two choices. She could quit her job now, walk away from all that money she desperately needed, or she could suck it up and fight the urge to kiss him again. *That is not going to be easy, maybe totally impossible.*

It wasn't love; it was lust, pure and simple. It's just a normal reaction to someone who was sexy as hell and could light a fire in her with just one touch. She needed to look at it solely as a sexual need and nothing more. *And it will never happen again.* He'd obviously had something troubling him that afternoon and was looking for a distraction. It didn't matter if it was her or some other woman. There was no reason they couldn't go back to the way things were earlier in the week. He stayed in the lab, and she avoided all contact. If she walked away from this job now, it would be another mistake to add to her ever-growing list.

Tomorrow started a fresh week. The countdown was already on to the end of the assignment. If she could pull this off, B&H Advanced Engineering was going to be a sweet addition to her résumé. A name like that could open doors to the businesses that most people wished they had access to. Landing this position, although temporary, carried a lot of weight as they were one of the most sought after chemical engineering companies in the world.

That rejuvenated her to make this a success. She had worked hard to gain the necessary skills, and this was the opportunity to prove she had what it took to be one hell of a personal assistant. Nothing was going to get in her way. She was in charge of her life, where it was going. No one was going to decide her future. *Not this time.*

Chapter Nine

GOING HOME WAS different than it had been in the past. Normally she returned to Boston feeling beaten down, as though she were a disappointment to her parents. Not this time. She wasn't sure what had changed. Was it possible time did heal all wounds, or had they all grown past the hurtful words they had said? The words were a blur now and didn't seem that important. *Let them stay that way.*

These last few weeks had brought a lot of changes. Some good and some she still wasn't sure about. Last night she'd spent hours debating them. Her choices around her family were some of them. Had staying away so long been a mistake? If it was, no one made her feel that way, at least not this time. It was not only good for her, but Nicholas loved having the run of the house, giggling like crazy as Nana chased him. A month ago she wouldn't have thought it possible. *Now anything is possible.* Her relationship with her parents wasn't perfect, but whose was? *Maybe that's where I've been wrong these past years. I wanted them to be perfect, even though I wasn't. So much wasted time. But no more. I'm a mother now; I know the reality of being a parent. Sometimes you might just get it wrong.*

After a good night's sleep, she was ready for whatever Brice was going to throw her way. Her confidence was strong, and she knew this week was going to be different. Lena exited the elevator and headed to her desk, ready for a new week. *Or so I thought.* The aroma of the fresh roses filled the room. Reluctantly she walked over to the beautiful red roses on her desk, searched for a card, but found none. It was odd, but she knew who they were from and preferred no card opposed to what he may have said on it. *Thanks for the afternoon delight.*

She wanted to pick them up and throw them into the wastebasket. Call him and tell him she didn't want his flowers or anything else he might offer. As she sat at her desk, she found herself staring at them. *Why did you send them, Brice?* Maybe he felt bad about what transpired last week, and this was supposed to be some form of peace offering. If so, she would prefer he ignore it and just move on. *Like I am trying to do.*

Taking the vase, she moved them to the filing cabinet, so they wouldn't be in her way while working. *Who am I kidding? I won't get anything done if they are sitting here, taunting me, a constant reminder of how good it felt to touch him again.*

She could tell herself it was purely a physical attraction, but if that were the case, the flowers wouldn't bother her. He used to bring her flowers all the time when they dated, but never red roses. Lena had never questioned it then, but now she found herself questioning every aspect of her life, even the smallest detail. It was a defense she'd erected so she'd never be hurt again. *To be human is to feel, and I'm no machine.*

With a deep sigh, she got up from her desk and went to make Brice's coffee. Once she was confident it was just as he liked it, she headed for his office. *Please be dressed today. My restraint isn't what it should be and probably never will be when I am around you.*

The door was slightly ajar. Knocking lightly, she stood there waiting. *No more surprise entries for me.* She knocked a second time. *No matter how much I enjoyed the view.*

Anticipating seeing him again, her lips curled and her mouth dried. When there was no answer the second time, she pushed the door open a bit wider. No sign of him. A bit more and she noticed his office was unoccupied. She approached his desk and saw a half-empty cup of coffee. *My lucky day. You've already come and gone.*

Although she tried to suppress it, an overwhelming feeling of disappointment flowed through her. All she wanted yesterday was to get back to normal. As normal as two people who were once lovers and pretended as though they never were—or would be again—could get. *Who am I kidding? It's never going to happen. Not after everything we've shared.*

Lena heard the phone ring at her desk. *And so it begins.* Forcing a smile, she left his office and closed the door. "Good morning. This is Mr. Henderson's office, Lena speaking. How may I help you?"

"Where's Nancy? Don't tell me that idiot brother of mine fired the best personal assistant he will ever have."

Well, thanks for the confidence builder there. "I'm only here temporarily." *Not that it's any of your business.*

"Hey, I hope I didn't come off sounding like a complete ass. That's usually Brice's job." His deep laugh echoed through the phone.

"Not at all," she lied. *Must be in the genes.*

"So, where is that dear brother of mine?"

Lena knew Brice was one of six. Which one this gentleman was, still wasn't clear. It really didn't matter, as Zoey was the only one on the "transfer call" list. *What a messed-up family. I can't picture what holiday gatherings must look like.*

"Sorry, Mr. Henderson is not available at this moment. I would be happy to take your name and have him call you." It was the same thing she said to almost every person who called. *I should get it on a recording and save time.*

"He has you trained already, does he? Don't answer that. We all know the game. Tell him Alex called. I can leave my number, but we both know he won't call."

Lena swallowed hard. She'd handled difficult callers many times, but this one left her feeling uncomfortable. What do you say when the person on the other end already knows the truth? *And it's not pretty.* "I'll give him your message." *And an earful of how to treat family, too.*

"I'm sure you will hear from him once he is free."

How had the person she once loved become so distant from everyone? She never would've given him a second date, let alone be with him for a year, if he'd acted like this. When they had been together, he'd made her laugh. He had always been serious about work and very driven for success, but when did it become the one and only thing he cared about? When had he become a stranger to his own siblings? She knew he'd cared about them as he had talked about them with pride back then. *What went wrong?*

Lena was tempted to ask him, but doing so would only open up conversations about their past. She had long since stopped asking herself why. Now *"What went wrong?"* was the question she asked herself daily. Was it time for her to get the answers to their sudden and harsh breakup? Would he even answer the question if she asked? And what difference would it make now if he did? *It only confuses things more. Going back won't change what happened.*

The phone rang again. "Good morning, Mr.—"

"Lena, it's Zoey. How are you?"

Unlike her brother, Zoey's voice was warm and welcoming. "I'm good. How about you?"

"Hanging in there. How is Brice treating you? Not giving you too much of a hard time, I hope?"

"Not at all." Lying came easily with this job. She did it all day. *And hated it.*

"Good. I was worried it might be a bit . . . awkward.

You know after you guys were involved and everything."

And here is where it becomes more awkward. "That was a long time ago." *Or Friday night, depending if hot sex in the office counts or not.*

"Well, I'm glad to hear it. So tell that brother of mine I am going to be there at noon for lunch. I don't want any excuses that he can't make the time for his one and only sister."

"I'll add you to his schedule."

"Thanks. It's worth the try, right? What's the worst thing that can happen? If he says no, we can do lunch and catch up."

Lena wanted to laugh, but she knew Zoey wasn't joking. She liked Zoey, and they were not far off in age either, but having lunch with the boss's sister, never mind who that boss was, wasn't a good idea. *Please don't blow this off, Brice.*

Unfortunately, her gut was correct. Zoey arrived on time for a lunch date, and Brice blew her off without hesitation, using the same excuse he used for everything: "I'm in the middle of something critical and can't break away."

Lena felt so bad, and Zoey was just standing at her desk, so when she said, or demanded, they have lunch together, there really was no way to back out.

Surprisingly lunch was more relaxing than she had anticipated. The conversation turned to things she felt comfortable speaking about: local events happening in Boston.

Lena had reached for her purse but knocked it and its contents to the floor, and that was when everything went sour.

Zoey, being the sweet and helpful person she seemed to be, immediately got up and started helping her pick up everything. Lena could feel her heart pounding in her chest as the words were spoken. "I didn't know you had a child. What's his name?"

Lena took the toy truck and children's book from her. *Lunch was a huge mistake. What have I done?* The last thing she wanted to do was talk about her son. Not to anyone, especially not someone close to Brice. Her personal life was exactly that, personal, and she didn't want anyone's opinion on what she should or shouldn't do. Not answering was only going to imply she was hiding something, so she had no choice but answer her. "Nicholas."

"I like the name. Guess I was wrong."

Lena arched a brow puzzled by her statement. "About what?"

Zoey smiled. "I heard something in Brice's voice the other day when we spoke. I thought . . . well hoped, that maybe the two of you had hit it off again, and maybe you were dating. I didn't know at that time that you already had someone else in your life."

Oh my God. I don't know what she thinks she heard, but it wasn't about me. Unless it was anger, then maybe it was me. I can't let anyone think there is anything going on between Brice and me. It will lead to questions I don't want to answer. "No. We're not seeing each other. That was a long time ago, and we have both moved on."

"Apparently you did if you have a son." Zoey finished her soda then said, "I'm not so sure about Brice. When he was dating you, he was a different person. He smiled, laughed, and was a joy to be around. I actually thought he was going to marry you. I've never seen him look at anyone like that, before or since."

Are you trying to kill me here because it feels a lot like a knife to the heart? "He is a very busy man. I'm sure once this project is complete things will be different. Back to the way they used to be." *Minus me.*

Shaking her head, Zoey continued, her voice no longer holding the upbeat tone it had earlier. "I don't think so. Something changed in a blink of an eye. He wouldn't say what it was, so I'd assumed it was your breakup. If that wasn't it, then I'm not sure if we will ever see the man we once knew."

Lena knew what that felt like. That breakup practically killed her, and she still wasn't the same person she was then. *And I'll never be again.* There were things that happened that permanently changed her. There were times she wished she could turn back time and fix whatever had gone wrong with them so maybe she could have her happily ever after. But if changing the past meant not having Nicholas, then she was okay with how things were.

"I don't know him that well anymore. But I do believe things will change after he completes what he is working on. The stress is evident by the hours he works."

"I hope so, Lena. So why don't we talk about something happy?" Zoey smiled, yet her smile was obviously forced. "Have you any pictures of your little one?"

If she said no, then Zoey would questions what type of mother isn't out there bragging about her son, and if she did, that would only encourage the conversation to keep going. Grabbing her cell phone, she pretended to look at the time. "Oh, my. I forgot the time. I need to get back to the office. There is a call I have scheduled, and I am going to be late." Getting up from her chair, she picked up her purse and put twenty dollars on the table to cover her sandwich. "I better run, but we will have to get together again soon."

Lena waved and quickly made her exit. Only when the brisk air hit her face did she realize she had been holding her breath. *Not doing that again.*

Chapter Ten

THE REST OF the week went off without issue. Brice stopped by her desk and asked how she was. He never mentioned the flowers, and she didn't either. She and Brice had reached a good spot. Pleasant to each other. As one would expect in any other job.

After her lunch with Zoey, she had to admit her mind frequently wandered back and forth between who Brice had been and who he was now. Every so often, a glimpse of what was could be seen in his eyes, when they were a soft gray, not so full of anger. But she knew Zoey was wrong. The change within him didn't have anything to do with not being with her. That change may have happened the day they broke up, but it had taken place even before she'd laid eyes on him. If his family didn't know the cause, how was she ever going to be able to figure it out? *It's none of my business. If he wants to be unhappy, that is on him. I don't care in the least.*

If only that were true. The sadness in Zoey's eyes as she spoke of her brother still troubled her. If Brice didn't care, then he needed to know others did.

Mustering all her confidence, she waited patiently for him to come by her desk for his coffee. Today was the day she would ask. What exactly wasn't yet clear, but she was going to ask him something.

Instead, that changed with an early call from Brice.

"No calls today. Absolutely no one. Understood?"

"Yes sir, Mr. Henderson." *A bit grumpier than usual. Glad you didn't stop by today.*

The rest of the morning went by quickly. It was almost noon, and she was about to head out for lunch. When the phone rang, she almost let it go to voice mail, but something in her said to take the call. "Good morning, B&H Advance Engineering, Mr. Henderson's office. How may I help you?"

"Nancy, where is he? He's not picking up his cell phone."

She didn't recognize the voice or the number. He also seemed so angry he hadn't noticed she wasn't Nancy. *We don't sound anything alike.* No matter who he was, she still wasn't going to transfer him, so he might as well get ready to leave a message like everyone else. She wasn't about to be bullied. Not by him or anyone else. "Excuse me, who's calling please?"

The man questioned, "Who is this?"

"My name is Lena, and I am Mr. Henderson's personal assistant."

"Since when?"

Really? Don't tell me this is another one of Brice's brothers because this is ridiculous. She wasn't about to divulge any information or play any of their games. *I should have let it go to voice mail.* Ignoring his question, she asked again but in a firmer tone. "And your name is?"

"Barrington. Asher Barrington."

Lena felt her heart drop into the pit of her stomach. *Brice's partner. Shit!*

She'd never met him before, but by his tone, she knew he wasn't a man to mess with. Even if he had been on the do not transfer list, she probably would have done so anyway. Thankfully, even though Brice and Asher were partners, he didn't seem to work out of this office. *Let's hope it stays that way.*

"Mr. Henderson asked not to be disturbed." Lena couldn't help it. She knew her voice trembled as she spoke and waited for the inevitable.

"Do you know who I am?"

Softly she answered, "Yes, I do."

The man's voice rose as he demanded, "Then transfer my damn call now."

Without any hesitation, she put the call on hold and rang the lab. It continued to ring. Lena didn't want to tell Asher Barrington that Brice would not take his call. She was positive it would end in being cursed out if not fired. *Come on. Pick up.* Thankfully he finally answered.

"I said no calls today." His voice was as gruff as Asher's.

What is wrong with everyone today? "Sorry. But he insisted."

"Lena I s—"

"Mr. Barrington is on line one." Then all was quiet. All she could do was wait. *Just take the call.*

"Put him through."

Thank God. Before she hung up, she hit the transfer button. *Oh, how I wish I could eavesdrop on this conversation. I'm sure it's going to be a heated one.*

"NEITHER OUTCOME IS acceptable." Brice couldn't believe it. *Dammit.* Not only did he carry the weight of the entire development and testing of this project on his shoulders, but now he needed to think about the business negotiations in Trundaie as well. *This is what you get when your business partner has the tact of Dominic Corisi.* "Asher, you need to reconsider your process and each component of it. Remove the unacceptable and reconfigure with a substitution." *One that doesn't involve violence and destruction maybe?* "Have you considered a more diplomatic approach?"

Even over the phone he could hear Asher's frustration. *If you didn't act like a bull in a china shop, maybe we wouldn't have these issues.* Brice grew up watching his father use this same heavy-muscle tactic to get whatever he wanted. It was lucrative, but what was his legacy going to be? *Take what you want. Crush what you can't have.*

Brice was equally driven but logical. He wracked his brain for the right answer. This wasn't his field of expertise. The only person he knew who had ever dealt with any kind of overseas disaster was Trent Davis in

Dubai, but the place was known for luxury, not turmoil. *And Trent's no sweet talker either.*

"Have you considered your brother Ian? He has a skillset that could be the third option you haven't considered. Perhaps a more diplomatic approach could convince the Trundaie government to step up in this situation. The rebels are their issue, not ours."

After the call, Brice wanted to do one thing, to focus on what he could control, his responsibility for the business, but that wasn't going to be possible until he knew for himself what the situation looked like. Opening his computer, he googled Trundaie. It looked like they were a country on the verge of revolution, something that had been building for years. Searching deeper, he came across something new. It was brief but powerful. A new rebel force threatening the destruction of an American-based company both in Trundaie and abroad. *That's B&H. Fuck.*

Brice now understood Asher's concerns. *This is more volatile than I thought.* What exactly had it meant by there and abroad? Asher mentioned hiring Bennett Stone as head of security. This facility was secure. This new addition didn't have anything do to with someone trying to steal his formula. That meant only one thing. *The stakes just got higher.* Did that mean personal threats against their lives? *And what about our families and friends?*

He closed his laptop again. He needed more answers, and not just the ones Asher provided. They had been friends since childhood, and he had spent more time at the Barrington's home than he had at his own during his younger years. Asher would do a lot of things, but he wouldn't risk his family. From what he remembered, they were all close with parents who watched out for the whole lot of them. Whatever was going on, he knew Asher would do whatever was required to fix it. *Even if I don't always agree with your business practices, I wouldn't want anyone else as a partner, Asher. Now fix this shit.*

The phone rang again. *What the hell! How am I going to get anything done, Lena, if you keep transferring calls?* "What now?"

"Ross Whitman is on the line. He said you were expecting his call."

He was, but that was before everything started going to hell. His intentions of finishing this project, taking a month off to sail the seas and regroup, were quickly vanishing. If he couldn't find a way to stay on track, no one would need to worry about what was happening in Trundaie because there wouldn't be a product ready for production. "Put him through."

"Brice, I wanted to let you know the boat is ready to go. Unless you have decided to throw a last-minute change in the mix, you can have your boat any time."

"Are you delivering it, Ross?"

Ross's laughter echoed through the receiver. "Since it is in sunny California I thought you might want to take it out. Especially after that winter from hell you've had in Boston this year."

After last week's arctic blast of cold, he would have jumped at the chance to take a break. But not only was there no time, right now everything was up in the air. He wanted that boat but it was, unfortunately, going to have to wait. "Hold on to it for a while. I'll be in touch when I'm ready."

"Great. Does this mean you are thinking of more changes? I know you like things exactly as you want them, Brice. I'm the same way. But your idea of a minor change isn't the same as mine. This boat is top of the line. The only thing it can't do is walk on land or fly, and if you need either one of those—"

"Fly you say?" It was Brice's turn to laugh. He *had* given Ross a hard time. Was it so bad he only wanted the best and wouldn't settle for anything less? If it was that way in his professional life, why should anyone expect anything less from him in his personal life?

"Sorry I mentioned it. I'll hold it here in port. If you need it delivered, let me know. I won't mind taking this baby out for an extended test ride with Jill."

"I'll be in contact, Ross. You just hold it there." If there was any test-driving, it was going to be done by him. In another two weeks, he would hand this project off to Asher and the plant foreman. Not entirely, but there would be a short break between completion on his end and the actual startup of production. Brice knew exactly how he wanted to spend that time. *Christening my new boat . . . with Lena.*

If he thought he would get any more work done today after that, he better think again. It was a total loss once he envisioned her lying naked on the deck in the moonlight as he touched and tasted every inch of her. His cock was already hard for her. *Maybe she would like a replay of last week.*

Throwing his lab coat over the back of his chair, he headed for her office. Hopefully, she didn't have any plans for dinner. *To hell with dinner, dessert sounds better.*

As he walked down the hall, he could hear her sweet voice as it softly echoed in the empty corridor. He could tell she was on the phone but couldn't make out with whom. As he came around the corner, her voice was loud and clear.

"I love you, baby."

What the fuck? His mood suddenly changed from a need for her to wanting to punch someone. At no point had she mentioned a boyfriend or significant other. *I never asked either.* Whoever it was, it couldn't be serious. *At least not so serious that she refused me.*

"Who was that?" Brice demanded.

"Sorry. That was a personal call. I'll try not to let it happen again."

"That's not what I asked." It felt like a storm was raging within him.

She looked puzzled for a moment then angry. "Do I understand you correctly? You believe you have the right to know my personal business?"

I want to know everything about you. Brice said nothing and waited for her response.

Lena stood up, crossed her arms in front of her, and said firmly, "Let me make one thing clear, Mr. Henderson. No one, including you, has any right to ask who I speak to or what I do."

"What you do on my property is my business. This is a secure facility for a reason. How do you know that your boyfriend is not using you to gain information about my project?"

Lena shook her head, raised her hand in protest, and responded. "I can guarantee you the person I was speaking to just a moment ago does not know anything about you or what you do. And trust me, I have absolutely no intention of ever mentioning your name to him."

He searched her eyes for some sign of what her feelings were for that guy. The only thing she revealed was a distaste for how he'd just spoken to her. *Get in line. I rub a lot of people that way. But I always get what I want in the end.*

He stepped closer, so she was only inches away. "Good. Keep it that way. What happens between us stays with us."

She swallowed hard and turned her eyes from his. "Bri—"

He reached out and stopped her, cupping her face in his hands, his thumb brushing against her soft lips. *God, I want her.* His lips claimed hers, and his tongue forced her lips to open to him. Her hands came up and pushed against his chest, trying to gain distance from him. That only enticed him to probe her mouth deeper with his tongue. Brice felt her resistance ease. Her hands were no longer pushing him away. Now she clung to him, bringing her hands up to his shoulders and pulling him to her.

His blood began to rush through his veins. Everything in him ached for release, but he needed to stop. What happened last week inside his office couldn't take place in the open. Not that he cared who saw what, but the security team downstairs watched everything. The only rooms not on camera were his and Asher's offices. There was no denying she wanted him, but he was sure she wouldn't forgive him for letting others watch.

"Lena," he said softly against her ear.

A sigh of pleasure escaped her lips, and she trembled in his arms.

Damn, you're not making this any easier. "Baby, if we don't stop now, I won't be able to later."

Her eyes met his, and then she looked around. Her beautiful olive skin glowed with the realization of her predicament. Lena pulled out of his arms and went back to sit at her desk, trying to act as though nothing had happened.

Brice reached out and took her right hand in his. Bringing her fingers to his lips, he placed a gentle kiss on them. "Have dinner with me."

Her eyes were still covered by her long dark lashes as she shook her head. "I can't."

"Why not?"

"I'm . . . ah . . . I'm meeting someone at six."

Was it the man she was professing her love to earlier? "You want to be with me." It wasn't a question. Her flushed cheeks weren't only from embarrassment.

When she spoke again, her voice could barely be heard. "It's too late, Brice. We can't go back."

"I'm not asking you to."

She finally raised her head to look at him. For the first time, he saw someone who was unsure. *Is it that you don't know what you want? Or who you want? I'll help you make that decision.*

"I'm . . . not the same person I was years ago. I've . . . moved on."

He heard the words, but they meant nothing to him. She may want to move on, but she hadn't. She was on fire when he touched her and met his kisses with her own. Whoever Lena thought she loved right now was only a sad replacement for him. *No competition.*

Letting her hand go, Brice headed to his office. Over his shoulder he said, "We'll leave at four. I'll make the reservation."

Chapter Eleven

S HE WAS HERE, but that didn't mean she was going to enjoy herself. If he wanted to be a controlling, arrogant ass, then she had no problem being a bitch.

The waitress came over to take their order.

"Water, please."

Standing there, pen in hand, she asked, "And for your entrée?"

Lena turned from the waitress and looked at Brice. Smiling, she answered, "Just water for me, thank you."

His expression changed briefly, and it pleased her that she'd caught him off guard. Was he so used to everyone bowing to his demands that no one ever said no to him? Well, he'd forgotten who he was dealing with. She'd challenged him back then, and since their breakup she'd gotten even stronger.

The well-trained waitress didn't comment. She turned to Brice. "And for you, sir?"

Brice continued to meet her gaze straight on. "Prime rib with a baked potato." When the waitress left, he asked, "Not hungry, Lena? I know you like their food;

we used to come here often."

She hadn't forgotten. In fact it was where he took her on their first date. When they pulled up to the restaurant, her heart sank as the memories came flooding back to her. She wondered if he had purposely chosen it as a form of torture or if had he had forgotten. Lena had her answer now and should have known before. Brice didn't leave anything to chance. He never forgot anything. But she wasn't about to play the game of Memory Lane. Holding her chin up in defiance, she stated, "I believe I told you I already have plans for dinner."

Lena expected him to ask about them, but he didn't. *Maybe he knows I'm not going to answer any of his questions about my personal life.*

"That's unfortunate. I believe your favorite dish here was the prime rib and, for dessert, a piece of lemon meringue pie." His grin said a lot. No matter how much she didn't want to be there with him, he apparently had every intention of enjoying his meal no matter if she ate or not.

The waitress delivered his food. Brice cut into it. It was perfectly cooked. Her mouth watered to sample such a treat again. The last time she'd eaten anything so decadent had been when they were dating. Being a single mother meant you made different choices. No longer would she drop fifty dollars for a meal when she could use that money for diapers and food for her son. Though she tried to ignore it, she found herself watching him lift the fork to his mouth.

"If you change your mind, I might let you have a bite of mine." Brice smiled before taking a succulent morsel into his mouth.

Damn you, Brice. Does everything have to be like this? An endless tease of something I can longer have? It wasn't a cut of meat that had her emotions tied up in knots. It was him, taking her to this place, back to a time where they were happy, in love, or so she had thought. His lack of understanding only confirmed her actions back then. Not calling him had been the right thing to do. Not telling him about her, but more importantly about Nicholas. Everything was his way or no way at all, and that was not how she wanted her son to live. To only have a father in his life when he chose to be there. No, he deserved so much better than what Brice would have been able to give him.

She felt sick keeping this from him, but he had made it very clear back then, no one, not family, not her, was more important than his damn job. Even this dinner had nothing to do with him wanting to be with her. It only had to do with control, and she wasn't about to fall for it. It would only lead to more pain than she could possibly bear.

Lena needed to stop thinking of him, of them, and their past. It would change nothing. Instead, she would hold to her promise to Zoey and mention how he had changed. *Let's see how you like being questioned, Mr. Henderson.*

"Your sister was very disappointed you blew her off

for lunch the other day."

"She's knows I'm busy."

"Yet you're not too busy to be sitting here with me, when you know I don't want to be sitting here with you." Folding her hands in front of her on the table she asked, "Why is that, Brice?"

He laid his fork down and stared at her. "Protest as much as you want, but you are here because you want to be."

Like hell I am. "You forced me to come," Lena said with a voice full of anger, both at him and at herself.

Brice leaned across the table and said softly, "I don't recall dragging you here, kicking and screaming."

"You're my boss. What was I supposed to say after I clearly told you I didn't want to go?"

He grinned. "So, what you're telling me is I hold all the power to make you do anything I wish because I sign your paycheck?" She didn't answer. "That's good to know because next time I'll invite you to have breakfast in bed with me." His laughter echoed through the room. "Would tomorrow work for you?"

When she went to tell him exactly where he could stick that offer, he raised his hand to cut her off.

"I'm joking, Lena. When did you become so uptight? Was it so long ago that you can't remember how to laugh and enjoy yourself when you're with me?"

I remember everything. I wish I didn't. "I don't think about the past. Like you, I only look toward the future."

"Good. What are your future plans with what's his

name?"

"Who are you talking about?"

He was watching her closely as he spoke. "The guy who sent you the roses. Was it his thank you for a good time over the weekend?"

They weren't from you? Who could they be from? There's no one. She would not give him the satisfaction of knowing that since their breakup, she'd been alone. Going out with Rex over the weekend had been the closest thing she'd had to a date in nearly three years, and that was a casual outing with an old friend. What she didn't understand was why Brice cared who she spent time with. He didn't want her, so why would he care if she found someone who did? Was it possible he was regretting how things ended between them? *God knows I do.* Was he hoping for a second chance to make it work?

Do I want a second chance with Brice Henderson? The old Brice had been everything she'd wanted in a man. He was brilliant. He'd been attentive, kind, focused, funny, and it would be a lie if she thought she'd experience anyone better in the bedroom. Now he was cold, volatile, and unpredictable, and seemed to have no concern about sleeping with her even if he thought she was with someone else. *Would he do that to me if I took him back? Sleep with another woman just because he wanted to?* Part of her wanted to take him back, but the decision didn't only affect her. Nicholas would be affected by whatever choice she made. Her feelings for Brice, whatever they were, needed to stay buried. She couldn't risk exploring them more than she already had. If he found out he had a son, it would end everything and possibly risk having to share custody with him. *That's never going to happen. Never.*

The only way to make sure was to let him believe there was someone else in her life. *But who is that person supposed to be? I'm home every night with my son.* Searching her list of friends she could ask to pretend to be her boyfriend was limited. Everyone male she knew was married or related. *Except Rex.*

"Have you forgotten his name already?" Brice accused.

"My relationship with Rex is none of your business." There. She said it. He has a name. Hopefully, now he can drop the questions. By the look on his face, she knew he was more adamant than ever. *Sorry Rex. Hope you forgive me for this.* "We had a wonderful time together this past weekend. Dinner, a movie—it was great. What did you do this weekend, Brice? Spend all your time in the lab?"

HE HAD ASKED but had hoped she didn't have an answer for him. Brice knew the flowers weren't for her birthday so it left only one thing: they were for something special. He use to bring her flowers but never bought roses; they symbolized of a lack of imagination.

Rex? What kind of name was that? Lena never had been one to run around, so spending the weekend with the guy meant they must have known each other for some time. He was tempted to ask her more about him, but she was only going to give him what she wanted him to know. Brice didn't have time to play games. However, Asher had just mentioned bringing on someone new as head of security. He had meant to give Bennett Stone a call himself regarding the status in Trundaie; he might as well add Rex to the list of things he wanted information on.

"My project is complete. I have time this weekend if you want to spend it with me." That was a total bold-faced lie. His formula was ready, but after the call from Asher, he had no idea what adjustments would need to be made. Asher had no concept that the formula needed adjustment based on temperature as well as altitude. If things weren't going as planned for Trundaie, he was not as close as he thought he was.

"Did you not hear me say I am seeing someone? Why would you ask me to spend a weekend with you when you know there is someone else?"

Because I want you. "Were you seeing him last Friday when you came to my office?" He knew his words were far from kind. But she couldn't tell him she loved this guy, Rex. Not after the way she touched him and gave herself to him that afternoon. No, that guy was nothing. If she thought otherwise, she was lying to herself, but then again he remembered she'd sounded sincere on the phone earlier.

Lena stood up abruptly. "How dare you speak to me like that?"

Brice looked at her and said, "Sit down." He wasn't about to apologize for what he said.

Lena looked around the room then sat down.

"Lena, I am not trying to interfere in whatever it is you have with this Rex. Do what you want. I don't care. But you didn't answer my question. Would you like to spend the weekend with me?"

He knew she wanted to, but she couldn't bring herself to agree to it. Was it embarrassment? They were adults who once were lovers. Why couldn't they continue to enjoy some mutual satisfaction? *God knows it's good between us. And I can't picture anyone making you feel as good as I can.*

She sat quietly for a moment. When she did answer, it wasn't a rejection. "Brice. Things are so complicated. Spending time together is only going to make things even more so. You only want me now because I'm here; it's easy for you. Once my assignment is through, and I'm gone, you will forget all about me again." Her voice was soft, and he could hear pain as she spoke the next words. "I can't go through that again, Brice. You might not remember how it ended the first time, but I'll never forget. You hurt me like no one else had. I waited and hoped you would call, but you didn't. You cut me out of your life. Don't ask me to let you back in now, especially not as some sexual play toy for you to enjoy whenever you want." She looked him in the eye. "Now if you will excuse me, as I mentioned, I have dinner plans and cannot keep him waiting." Getting up, she said softly,

"Let's forget Friday ever happened. It was poor judgment on both our parts."

He didn't try to stop her. She was right; he had been an asshole back then. It had not been a great time of his life, and he wasn't proud of his past behavior. Brice had been so focused on his project that when his father gave him the ultimatum, he lost his mind and had cut everything and everyone who meant anything to him out of his life.

It hadn't been an easy choice, but at the time, it was all he had been able to do. If he had stayed with her at that time, she would have spent her nights and weekends alone, waiting for someone who wasn't coming. He needed to focus all his energy to make B&H one of the most powerful companies around. He felt guilty for the way he'd broken things off, but he would feel worse if she had spent the last three years sitting around waiting for him.

The thought that she was with another man pissed him off, but it was better than her being alone. He had had lovers since her as well, but they'd only provided a release for his sexual tension, nothing more. Lena had never been that person to him. Not then and not now. *Hell, I don't know what you are to me now, but you've got me tied in knots.*

There was only one problem. He'd heard her on the phone. Her voice, when she'd said those three words, had been spoken in truth. She loved that guy. *But we'd had sex on Friday.* Only a complete asshole would ignore that and pursue her anyway. Getting up from the table, he threw money down to cover his tab and walked out. *Good thing I'm an asshole.*

Chapter Twelve

HIS CALL WITH Bennett last night wasn't what he'd hoped to hear. Asher had spoken as though he had everything under control. How that was possible after only a week with a country on the verge of a revolution was beyond him. It looked more likely that their plan B of setting up in New Hampshire was going to be their best option. *This isn't what I would want in my backyard if something goes wrong at the plant.*

The plant wasn't his only concern at this moment. Bennett mentioned the threat made against Asher and him. Normally he wouldn't give a damn. But he hinted the threat could impact people around them. "Slim chance for domestic retaliation," was how he'd put it. Brice wasn't exactly sure what this rebel group was willing to do in order to gain support, but he didn't want to find out. *The only world news I want B&H to make is for positive investment opportunities.*

He didn't like the idea of having anyone watching him, but it looked like it was time to make exceptions to his rules. He increased security around the building as well as his personal property. Also gave his brothers the heads-up. Like him, they were used to watching their backs all the time, mostly because their father was always waiting for his moment to break them. Dean, as usual, wouldn't take what he said seriously. He only laughed and said, "No problem. I'll hire myself a hot sexy security guard, and we won't leave my bedroom until this all blows over."

Zoey wasn't someone he could call to deliver this message. She was much more fragile than she was ever going to admit. No, it required taking her to lunch and breaking it to her gently. This would in turn mean getting yelled at for his careless behavior. *It wasn't the first time, and it sure won't be the last.*

Before meeting with Zoey, there was one more person he needed to have a conversation with. He was sure she would think this was some ploy to come between her and Rex, but that wasn't the case. He didn't need to make up a threat. He was enough threat himself when it came to them.

Hitting the intercom button he said, "Lena, come into my office."

She entered, carrying her notepad. "Do you need something?"

I need you. "Sit. There is something we need to discuss."

Lena looked at him, hesitating to come closer. He didn't blame her. The last time she'd approached his desk had been explosive to say the least.

"This is business." Brice wanted to ease her mind. She was going to have enough to deal with, and if he was going to get her to see the actual issue at hand, she needed to trust him. *And that's not going to be easy.*

Lena took the chair opposite him. "What is it you wish to discuss with me?"

"I know you only have a week left of this assignment. You have filled Nancy's shoes surprisingly better than expected."

Smiling, Lena replied, "I am glad I had the opportunity. If it's not too much to ask, I was hoping you might consider writing me a letter of recommendation for future work."

He hadn't really thought about her leaving. Nancy was about to return next week, and he couldn't have two personal assistants. Lena was good, but brought a level of distraction he wouldn't want on a daily basis. At least not in the office. "I am sure that can be arranged. But that's not why I asked you in here. Something has come up with the location of the plant, and our security team feels it would be wise if we took some additional precautions."

He watched as Lena's face filled with concern. Rightly so, too. "Are we safe here?"

"You will notice additional security in place. These men can be trusted. I have to ask you not to leave the building during the day. Lunch will be provided for all the staff, and I will give you the contact to make all these arrangements."

"This is serious, isn't it?"

"We don't know yet. Our head of security is working closely with Asher Barrington to see if we can save this plant in Trundaie, or if we need to pull out. Until we know the threat has ceased, we all need to have eyes in the back of our heads. Anything unusual, I want you to call me immediately. Understood?" He didn't want to panic her, but he'd rather she be scared and safe than to let anything happen to her. *I lost you once. I'm not letting you go a second time.*

"I understand. Can you tell me if we should feel concerned outside of the workplace? I mean, at home?"

"I don't know." He walked around the desk and sat on the edge, facing her. "Lena, I know this is more than you expected when you took this job. Whether you want to believe it or not, I care about you and won't let anything happen to you. I have assigned a security team to watch your apartment and will monitor you wherever you are until this settles down." Her eyes widened and by the quick intake of breath, he could tell she was frightened.

"Why do you think they would come after you and not Asher?" There was a definite tremor in her normally confident voice.

"We are both at risk, but I am the chemist who created this product. They might not want us in their country, but that doesn't mean they don't want our technology."

Lena sat twisting her fingers, obviously nervous. "I need to take the rest of the afternoon off. I am sorry for the short notice, but there is something I need to take care of if you don't mind."

She was shaken more than he had anticipated. "Stay with me at my house. You will not need to worry there. No one is getting in unless I say so."

Lena shook her head. "It's not me I'm worried about. He—" She stopped and rose from the seat. "There's more than just me I need to worry about."

All he could do was watch as she walked out of the office. His blood began to boil. He offered her the safety of his home, and yet all she could do was think about Rex and his well-being. *Rex should fear me, not the rebels from Trundaie.* She cared about *him* more than her own well-being. *You better be worth it, Rex, because if you hurt her, your ass is all mine.*

She had never packed things so quickly in her life. Thankfully it was only Nicholas's clothes and toys she needed to worry about. Her mother was ecstatic about watching him for a week; she never even asked why. Good thing because it would've only meant telling her she couldn't go back to Boston either.

It was still early in the day when she arrived. March provided hope for spring, and they had nice weather in Plymouth. She had decided to take advantage of what was left of the day and do something she couldn't do back in Boston. Lena spent the afternoon chasing her son through the park until they were both exhausted.

If Nicholas couldn't be with her, then the next best

thing was him being with her parents, safe and sound. She could take care of herself, but protecting Nicholas was her first priority. *And always will be.*

Lena stayed as late as she could to make sure everything was going to be okay. It was the first time she was leaving her son overnight anywhere. But this wasn't with just anyone. It was with her parents, the same ones who'd protected her and would now do so for her son.

Since no one in Boston knew of Nicholas, there should be no threat here. If she left her job suddenly, it might spark some interest that she had the information they wanted and they'd follow her. Now she would be able to return to Boston and rest easily. *As easy as I can when he's not with me.* Nicholas was tucked in bed before she left, and her lips lingered on his sweet cheek when she kissed him goodbye. Her parents had put him to bed for her but this wasn't going to be for only a few hours. He was going to wake up without her too. For the first time since she had him, she was going to be alone. *He's probably going to handle this much better than I will.*

Lena had expected to take the bus back, but somehow Rex had heard she was back in town for a few hours and had managed to get invited to join them at the house for dinner.

"After all that coffee, I'm not going to sleep for hours, so let me drive you back. It will give us some time to talk."

"Rex, are you sure? It'll be a long ride back by yourself." Although she was grateful not to have to ride the bus or enter her home alone, she also didn't want to worry about another person. Her list was growing too quickly, and she already had enough on her plate.

"I'm going to visit a friend while I'm there and won't be coming back tonight either." She looked at him questioningly. "What? Do you think you're the only one who knows people in Boston?"

She couldn't help but laugh. Even though she didn't have romantic feelings for Rex, she was glad to have him as a friend. Maybe the trip would give her time to express how she felt about him. The last thing she wanted to do was lead him on and break his heart. *God knows I know how that feels, and it sucks.*

Chapter Thirteen

*W*HERE THE HELL *are you, Lena?* For the third time, his call went directly to her voice mail. *Are you in trouble or just avoiding me?* The way he spoke to her the other day, he wouldn't be surprised if she had blocked his number for good. When he checked with the guard he had placed at her apartment, he had been told she wasn't there. Lena had asked for the day off to take care of something; he wished he knew what the hell that something was.

A few weeks ago everything had been on target. Not only with the project, but where he wanted to go in life. Ever since he opened his office door and saw her standing there, his life seemed to be put on hold, as though in limbo. Looking back now, he couldn't remember why he'd never picked up the phone and called her. He had meant to, but somehow time got away from him and before he knew it, months turned into years. The anger she felt toward him was well deserved. If any man treated his baby sister like he had Lena, Brice would probably be up for assault charges. So what right did he have asking her to look toward the future when he never explained what had happened in the past? *Is that what I want? A future . . . with Lena in it?*

No one truly knew the level of danger, but something inside him needed to protect her. The threat against her was minimal, so why did he let her believe it was much greater than it was? *Because I want her close to me. And only me.*

Since she wasn't home, he could only guess she was with Rex. *You run to him for the comfort you can't find with me.* He could feel his pulse pounding in his temple. Knowing they were together wasn't sitting well with him at all. Brice needed to find out who this Rex was, and maybe then he would understand why Lena seemed willing to risk her life to be with him. *No one is worth that. Not even me.* Brice couldn't picture Lena being forthcoming with Rex's last name, so he was going to need to become a bit more creative when it came to obtaining the information he required.

Brice typed an email with the details about Lena and the only piece of information he knew, his first name: Rex. *Bennett, you're supposed to be the best, let's see if you can deliver.*

He knew that wasn't what Bennett had been hired for, but once he was on the payroll, his job became anything Brice said it was. No different than any other employee.

He wasn't sure how long it would take to hear back but if he was as good as Asher said, it shouldn't take him long. Besides, Lena still had another week of employ-ment, and he couldn't picture her quitting at this point. *And even if you do, that's not going to stop me from getting what I want.* Running on adrenaline alone for months, his need for a hot, ready woman beneath him was great. *Why won't any woman do? Why Lena?*

He had spent many hours in his father's silent hospi-tal room fulfilling his obligations as requested by his sister. Left with nothing but his own thoughts, he'd tried to shut down his mind, yet the memories haunted him there. Each time he left with more questions than answers. *Thirty-eight and even in a coma, Dad, you still have a way of making me feel . . . unworthy.*

Nothing had come easy in Brice's life, and he didn't expect that to change. He was willing to fight for what he wanted just like his father had done before him. The difference was what they wanted and the means they used to get it. His actions lately were not something he was proud of. They reminded him of his father. Lena didn't want to talk about Rex. He could've respected her privacy. *That wasn't fucking happening. There is something in her eyes when she's quiet. I know she's thinking of him. Dammit. What is it about him? I need to know.*

Still sitting in his lab, he stared at a blank screen. Normally this would be a place he felt at ease, a place where he could shut out the rest of the world, but he found it impossible tonight. The harder he tried, the more difficulty he had concentrating, which lead to error after error. *Everything I touch turns to shit.* He had long ago given up getting any work done but wasn't yet ready to go home. There was nothing waiting for him there except a cold, empty bed. *The one I want to warm with Lena.*

There was more on his mind than having her again. Her lack of response to his messages worried him. Before he could rest, he needed to know she was okay. If anything happened to her because of this project . . . *Don't even go there, Brice. Nothing will happen.*

He was banking on Bennett and Asher to handle what he couldn't. It wasn't easy for Brice to relinquish control to another, but he had no choice. He had to trust they were taking care of what needed to be done in Trundaie. No different than Asher was counting on him to handle everything here. *Even if that means I make some enemies in the process.* There were times that being raised by a man who took no prisoners came in handy when it came to business. *This is going to be one of those times.*

His cell phone buzzed with a new text message. "She just arrived at her apartment."

About fucking time. Pushing away from his desk, he grabbed his coat and headed out the door. They had some unfinished business to discuss. The only way to ensure no harm would come to her was for her to stay at his home. Brice had offered once, and she'd refused. He couldn't afford to spend any more time worrying about her safety.

When he arrived at her apartment complex, he was glad he had a guard watching her. *She should have one all the time, living here.* It wasn't the best part of Boston. Many of the buildings had their first-floor windows boarded up, and the walls and street signs were plastered with graffiti. *Why does she live here?* When they were dating, she lived on the south side. Easy access to everything, and you felt comfortable walking the streets even at night. That was not the case here. He wasn't afraid, but a beautiful woman like her . . . He could only imagine how she must be harassed during the day, never mind getting home after dark like she did tonight.

How could her boyfriend let her stay here? He knew one thing for sure. As long as she worked for him, she wasn't staying here. Whether she liked it or not, she was about to pack some of her belongings and stay with him. *And I'm not taking no for an answer this time.*

LENA SAT ON the couch, her cheeks wet with the tears that were still flowing, because when she arrived home, it hit her. This was the first night she would spend without Nicholas. She was sure he was doing better than she was at this moment. *At least I hope so, baby boy.*

How she wished she could FaceTime with him, but once he was asleep, he was usually down for the night. Calling at this late hour would only worry her parents and possibly wake Nicholas. No, she would wait until morning. *It's going to be a long, rough night.*

Sniffing, she got up and started to charge her cell phone. Lena couldn't believe her battery had died on the trip home. If it weren't for the fact that Rex dropped her off on her doorstep, she would have been worried walking the streets without any way to call for help.

The ride with Rex had been amazing. Her first thought was how she could bring up that she only wanted to be friends. Fortunately on the way, he informed her that his friend in Boston was a woman he had a date with tomorrow night.

Lena wasn't sure what it was about Rex, maybe she just needed someone to talk to, but she found herself spilling her guts about everything that happened three years ago with Brice, and how she never told him about Nicholas. *Not that I hadn't intended to.*

Rex didn't judge her; he only listened. And the advice he gave her was something she already knew. *I need to tell Brice.*

But she couldn't do it right now. It's not like she could say: *Brice, you have a child, but because you put me at risk, he is now with my parents, and you need to stay away so no harm will come to him.*

She had one week left with this job, then she could tell him. At least this way if he still didn't want any part of a family he never had to see either one of them again. But until she was certain Brice wasn't going to hurt her son emotionally as he had her, she wasn't going to say a word to him. *Even if it's the right thing to do. I have to think of Nicholas first.*

Lena went to lie on her sleeper sofa. Tonight she didn't bother to open it. She was exhausted from the stress of the day. Pulling the blanket up to cover her bare legs, she closed her eyes and began to doze off.

Was it her imagination or was someone knocking on her door? *Please go away. I'm not answering. Just go.*

Lena didn't like her living arrangements, but it was all she could afford with her income. That's why the job at B&H meant so much. She was making in one month what she made in the entire year last year. It brought her one step closer to leaving the rat-infested hellhole she lived in and moving to a safer neighborhood. *One where I don't need to carry mace.*

The knocking continued. Lena looked to make sure she had bolted the door. Lying back down, she pulled the blanket over her head.

"Lena, open the door."

Brice? What the hell was he doing here? How does he know where I live? She didn't want to answer, but obviously, he wasn't going to leave until she did.

Getting up, she wrapped the blanket around her and opened the door. "What are you doing here?"

He pushed past her, and she watched as he scanned the apartment. "Are you alone?"

Does he know about Nicholas already? The look on his face was not one of anger but something else. She couldn't pinpoint it.

When she didn't answer, he asked, "Is he here? Your boyfriend?"

Lena understood his mood. He was jealous, but why? He didn't want her, so why did he care if someone else did? She had spent too many nights trying to guess what made Brice Henderson tick. She had no answers then, and she wasn't about to start searching for them now. "I'm alone. Is that why you're here?"

He shook his head. "I'm here for you. Pack your clothes, you're coming with me."

Her mouth gaped open in shock. Brice had always been demanding but never like this. She had no intention of leaving with him. She might not like where she was staying, but it was her home. "I'm not going anywhere with you, Brice. We discussed that earlier. What makes you think I will change my mind now?"

"Because you want to continue your employment. I am not paying for an entire battalion of security that would be needed to keep you safe here."

Lena was insulted. "Who do you think you are that you can come into my home and tell me what I need to do?" Brice stepped closer to her. She looked around to see if she had left any of her son's toys around. Thankfully she had packed them all with Nicholas's things. There was no sign of anyone living in the apartment but her. *A toy truck would be a sure giveaway.*

"Lena, I'm only going to say this once. You can pack your things and come with me willingly, or I can throw you over my shoulder and carry your ass to the car. But know this, you are coming with me."

His eyes burned into her. She shivered, but not in fear, because she knew he would never hurt her, but his forcefulness was still unnerving. Everything in her wanted to slap his face, tell him to get out, scream for help, but she knew none would come. She didn't want to go, but she knew there wouldn't be any place safer for her than with him. "You are such a prick, Brice Henderson."

She hated being told what to do, but a part of her actually appreciated the fact Brice had truly cared enough to come get her. *Is my life really in danger? How has my life become this roller coaster of crazy?* He was a prick, a gorgeous, sexy, self-absorbed prick. She couldn't help but feel thankful amidst her anger. *At least he isn't seeing any evidence of Nicholas.*

Lena dropped the blanket, grabbed her jeans that she'd tossed on the chair, and slipped them on. The only suitcase she owned was now at her parents. Opening a drawer, she pulled out a white kitchen trash bag and began to fill it with a few items. She had no idea how long he expected her to stay, but if she needed more, she would have to come back later. Right now there was only one thing on her mind. *Get out of here before he finds out about Nicholas.*

Chapter Fourteen

LENA DIDN'T SPEAK the entire ride. There wasn't anything to say. *Nothing nice at least.* The thought of staying at Brice's house didn't appeal to her, but she was grateful not to be alone tonight. Under any other circumstance, she might have looked forward to the company.

She sat quietly, looking out the window, refusing to even turn slightly in his direction. *Let my silence say what I feel.*

To her surprise they were leaving the city. She had no idea where they were headed. When they'd dated he'd had a penthouse apartment in Boston, and she couldn't picture him living anywhere else. It didn't take long before she saw the exit sign for Cambridge. That area wasn't known for apartments. Had he finally settled down and actually purchased a house? *But he's never there. Why would he do that?*

The last thing Lena wanted to do was spend more time trying to figure out Brice. They had been together for more than a year, and everything she thought she knew then had been wrong. The person she cared about would never have said the things he had. Not then or now. *What happened to the man I loved? What caused him to change so drastically and quickly?* They were compatible then. Now, they were as different as night and day. He had turned cold and controlling while she had become nurturing. *Maybe because I had to be. Is that why you changed? Did something happen that required you to become so hard and distant?*

Lena was no longer looking out the window but was now staring at Brice. He was leaning back against the limo's leather seat, his eyes closed, his breathing shallow. Confident that he was asleep, she looked at him more closely, something she hadn't allowed herself to do these past few weeks. The last thing she needed was for him to think she was interested in him in any way other than as her boss. *Of course having sex with him might have given him the wrong idea. Way to go, Lena.*

As he slept she adjusted herself in her seat so she could see his face. Nothing about him was relaxed. Even his jaw was still tense; she could see stress written all over him. *What have you gotten yourself into?* It wasn't her place to ask, but she had the feeling he was going through this alone. Maybe if he had someone to talk to, to vent to, it would help ease his tension.

The way Brice had been treating people, she wouldn't be surprised if he didn't have friends. Talking to family wasn't always the best choice either, because they have long memories, and when you least expect it, they remind you of your failures. *Time and time again.*

That's why talking to Rex earlier had felt so good. Someone to listen, for no other reason than he wanted to. No personal agenda. It was refreshing. If it weren't for that conversation, she probably would have laid into Brice when he showed up at her apartment. But instead she was able to see things from a different point of view. Brice might have his faults, but so did she. Keeping Nicholas a secret was a mistake. Not only for her son, but also for Brice. From what she saw all he had was B&H. There was no one special in his life, no one waiting for him when he got home. He might be one of the richest men in Boston, but she wouldn't trade places with him for anything. *I'd be so lonely.*

Should she tell him now or was the timing off? He had so much going on between his project and whatever issue he was dealing with at the plant he mentioned. How would he take the news he had something else to worry about?

No, this wasn't the time, but it would have to be soon. The longer this went on, the worse it was going to be when she finally did tell him. For now, she would be there to help him get through whatever he was dealing with. That is the least she could do for the father of her child.

HE MUST HAVE been more exhausted than he thought. Sleeping in the car wasn't something he ever did. After the last few days, however, it was desperately needed.

Waking to find Lena watching him, or more like studying him, made him want her even more. He didn't take her to his home to have sex with her; she was here so she would be safe.

You just keep telling yourself that bullshit, Brice, and maybe you'll start to believe it. He wanted her; that wasn't the issue. But she was something he didn't deserve to have: loving, gentle, kind, and happy. That wasn't who he was. For a short time he had been that person when he was with her, but it wasn't who he really was.

His father reminded him during their argument what a fucked-up individual he was. Lena had often spoken of her family, her childhood, and it had sounded so normal. *So happy.* A mother and father who loved her, brothers who watched out for her. Yes, she'd spoken of them like they were all too protective of her, not letting her live her life the way she wanted, but he knew by listening to her stories that it hadn't been out of wanting to control her, it was out of love.

The closest thing he had ever experienced to what a normal interaction was in a family was the time he spent at Asher's house when they were young. They'd sat down at family dinners and had spoken about their day. There had been no barking of orders. Instead there had been laughter and parents who'd seemed to love each other. *Funny, Asher acts more like he was raised by my family than his. Maybe my bad behavior rubbed off on him.*

That last thing he wanted was to continue the family chain and expose a child to the life he grew up in. It might not be as bad, but he wasn't going to risk it. That was the problem with being around Lena. She made him want what he shouldn't. Believe in things he couldn't have. The only time he ever thought of having a family was when they were dating. That was when he had purchased this house in Cambridge. It had been his intention to ask her to live with him. *That was right before I fucked it all up and kicked her out of my life.*

He might want her, need her, but God knows he didn't deserve her and never would. Brice would keep her here and protect her until he heard from Bennett that the threat had been eliminated. *But who is going to protect her from me?*

She should be treated tenderly and loved. What did he know of such things? Nothing in his childhood resembled love. Everything his father taught him was anything but love. *If you can't have it, crush it so no one else can.* Not the pep talk one would expect from a parent, but then again, his father was unique. Even in such poor health, the doctors said he fought all treatment. *It's always on his terms even it if means it may cost him his life. He'll never change.*

He may not be his father, but he couldn't run from his past either. He could see it in Lena's eyes when she looked at him. Was it fear or lack of respect for who he had become? *She knows I will never hurt her.*

When he was with her it was a constant internal battle, his old self trying to resurface. He couldn't afford to let that happen. If he did, he would be lost and would never be able to let her go again. She had moved on, found someone who made her happy. If Rex was that man, then he was going to have to accept it. *Yeah, that ain't ever gonna happen.*

As the limo pulled up to the house, he turned to Lena and said, "You'll be safe here. Make yourself at home; the staff will get you anything you need. I have to go back to the lab."

He opened the door so she could get out. She looked as though she wanted to tell him something, then closed her mouth, and got out of the car. The driver carried her "bag" to the door and let her in.

Brice knew he should go in, show her around, make her feel comfortable, but he knew if he was alone with her tonight, he wouldn't be able to stop himself. He needed to keep her safe; he had to stay away.

Chapter Fifteen

S HE STAYED UP as late as she could that night, waiting for Brice to return. He didn't. What was the point of taking her to his home if he wasn't going to be there with her? She wasn't entirely alone as there was a guard at the gate and anything she wanted or needed would be delivered to her with just one touch of a bell.

The only thing I want, I can't have right now. My son. Her normal morning routine would have been spent preparing everything for daycare. It felt odd having all this extra time. Grabbing her cell phone, she called her mother on FaceTime.

"Good morning, Lena. Is everything okay?"

Missing my baby. "Yes, everything is good. I wanted to check on Nicholas before I leave for work."

She heard her mother yawn. "He is still sound asleep; how about you call him on your lunch break?"

Lena wasn't worried. If she didn't need to be up so early, she wouldn't be either. "I'll call you when I have a break. The office can be a bit noisy at times." She'd already had one close call when saying goodbye, she didn't want Brice to catch her twice.

"Your father is planning on taking him to the dock today to watch the boats. Why don't we call you tonight before he goes to bed?"

Oh, I wish I was there too. The next generation, but the same ritual. Her father must be in his glory. When she first asked if they could watch Nicholas for a few days, she was worried it would be too much for them. From the sound of her mother's voice, this was a special time for them, and she was glad it was working out. *I wish it were under different circumstances.*

All she wanted to do was hide away from all the things that were waiting for her in the office. Lena pulled the blanket back over her head and let out a long sigh. *Why can't it be Saturday?* Wishing wasn't going to make it happen. Besides, lying in bed wasn't going to change anything. Brice said he would give her a letter of recommendation. That was going to come in handy no matter where her next job was. So she couldn't blow it, not with only this week left.

Dragging herself from the comfort of the guest bedroom, she searched for an outfit that wasn't a mass of wrinkles. *Why didn't I hang these up last night?* Probably because putting them away was conceding to Brice's demands. As long as they remained in her bag, then she felt as though she held some level of control. *No matter how little it was.*

Being here however had its advantages, the door-to-door service to work. No crowds, no waiting. That was something she could get used to. Lena expected to find Brice at work. Surprisingly he wasn't. There was a note on her desk that said he could be reached on his cell phone for emergencies only. No more details.

With everything going on, you'd think you might want to drop me a hint as to where you are. She knew he didn't need anyone to take care of him, as he was pretty damned intimidating, but if someone was really out to hurt him, she wanted—no needed—to know he was okay.

They might not be a couple any longer, but he was the father of her son and would always be someone special to her because of that. What she didn't understand was why he was so protective of her. It would make sense if he knew about their son, but he didn't.

How could she understand him, and why he was doing this now when she still didn't know why he left her so suddenly before? *Why can't you see it? No one has hurt me more than you did.*

Thinking back on the pain, she realized why it hurt so much. It was because of how deeply she had loved him. Maybe that's why she now kept her distance from everyone: her family, her friends, or any possible intimate relationship. The only one she let in was her son, and that was because she couldn't give him what he needed without letting him love her back.

Was just being so close to Brice again bringing down the walls she had struggled so hard to build? Was this what might lie ahead for her? More pain and heartbreak?

It didn't matter; she knew once this job was complete she would need to tell Brice everything. Of course, she also had her own set of questions for him. This had gone on too long, but it wasn't all her fault. She made the best decision she could. At any time he could have picked up that phone, called her, and she would have told him. Even now, the only reason they were speaking was because some head-hunting agency reached out to her, offering her a temporary assignment. It was only a coincidence that he owned the company. Otherwise, she wouldn't be contemplating *if* or *when* to tell him.

No matter when or how she said it, it wasn't going to go well. They said you should just rip it off like a Band-Aid, quickly. She was positive that didn't apply when telling a person they had a child. Especially when he had made it clear he wanted nothing to do with a family. The fact that the child was a two-year-old son, and he didn't know the word dada, wasn't going to help either. *Maybe this is fate and the timing is right and things will work out.* She shook her head. *Or the little world I have made for myself and Nicholas is about to get really ugly.*

It always ended the same, no matter how many times she played it out in her mind. He would be beyond angry at her and wouldn't forgive her for what she did. *If that's the way it plays out, then so be it. At least he will know. What he does with that information is all on him.*

The day had flown by and thankfully, with Brice out of the office, she was able to get in touch with her mother several times to check on her son. He had been either napping or out playing. "He is such a joy to have around. You really should move back to Plymouth so we can see more of him."

She had been waiting for that comment since she'd visited. It had been the last thing she wanted to do, move back to her hometown. Knowing all the freedom her son had, and being surrounded by family that loved him, it might be time to reconsider her living arrangements. *Maybe not all the way back to Plymouth, but closer, more rural.*

It was funny that she had achieved recognition for her skills as a personal assistant and most likely would land a job that would pay more than she dreamed of, but playing with her son in the park made her miss the quieter life. The family life.

Maybe once Brice knew the truth, and they worked out their issues, they could learn to be friends again and perhaps even more. She laughed out loud. *Yeah. That's never going to happen. I'll be lucky if he doesn't hate me.*

The stress of confessing now or later was causing her temples to throb. There was only another week of work. Could she pull it off until then? *I've got to. There's no way he is going to let me continue working for him once he knows.*

What should have been a relaxing day with Brice out of the office was anything but. Between the phones ringing off the hook and having to blow everyone off, she also was concerned because he'd never called to check in. He told her about the threat, but there couldn't be that big of an issue, could there?

There was only one way to find out. *Google it.* Lena spent the rest of the day searching articles about Trundaie. *As bright as you are, Brice, you decide to build a plant in a country that has been on the verge of revolution for over five years?* She closed the laptop and shook her head. *And yet you looked so surprised that it's not safe now. I think you should come out of the lab more often.*

SINCE LENA REENTERED his life, nothing had gone as planned. Before, he could tell you what his day looked like from dawn to dusk. Now nothing seemed ordinary. He knew it wasn't her fault. She hadn't caused the issues in Trundaie, nor had she made his father ill. Her presence was amplifying the issues around him. He couldn't think clearly when she looked at him with her sultry dark eyes.

His fuse was shorter than ever. The staff seemed relieved when he told them he wouldn't be in. *Enjoy it now. Tomorrow it's back to normal.* Whatever that meant now. He was angry at Nancy for taking the time off when he needed her most. Yes, Lena was doing an excellent job, he would give her that, but she also was giving him something he didn't need. *A distraction from what is important to me, B&H.*

After sleeping in his office last night he was able to think more clearly. Also getting the answers he needed from Bennett regarding Rex felt good too. He was someone she had gone to school with back in Plymouth.

Small-time restaurant owner who had no interest in leaving Plymouth again. That eased his mind. One thing he knew hadn't changed about Lena was her drive for success. She loved the city life and knew it was the place for her. Even when they were dating she never took him home to meet her family. She had said they didn't agree with her lifestyle. He could relate to that. His father never agreed with one damn thing he'd done. *I probably wasn't even born the way you wanted me to be.*

Brice opened his eyes and looked at his father. Why he had agreed to stay here was beyond him. *So what if you wake up, Dad? Seeing me isn't going to make you feel any better. It'll probably finish you off.*

The sign in the room said no cell phones so he was trapped with a man who was unconscious. *At least we're not fighting.* What he didn't understand was why Zoey insisted someone always be here. *It's not like he was there for us. But I'm not ready for him to die.* Any other time he would have told Zoey no, he was too busy. Today it was good to be away from the office. He needed to think, and that wasn't easy around Lena.

It was already dark, and his brother Dean should be arriving soon. *Can't blame him if he bails. This is why they pay nurses, so we won't have to sit here.*

"Brice." He heard his name mumbled from across the room. His father was awake. No matter what past they may have shared or how he tried to deny it, he was relieved. Getting up, he walked to stand by his father. His eyes were closed, but the monitors were beeping like crazy. Had it been his imagination?

The nurse came into the room and began pressing buttons. She was followed by a second nurse who rattled off instructions before turning to him. "Sorry, Mr. Henderson. We need you to wait outside, please."

He didn't move. Whatever was going on, he wasn't leaving. He might not deserve it, but the man was still his father, and if he was going to die, it wasn't going to be in a room filled with strangers. He should have his family with him.

Before he knew it, doctors had entered and were administering medication into his IV. With all the noise, he didn't know how any of them could hear the other, yet they worked as a precision machine. Each doing exactly as the other needed. Through it all he gained a new appreciation for life. They didn't know his father, yet they were doing everything in their power to save him. Guilt filled him as he stood back and watched. Only a few minutes ago he was hoping the waiting would be over, that there were better places he wanted to be.

It wasn't his imagination. He knew his father called out to him before having another attack. Was Zoey correct? Had he been asking for him all this time? If so, why? They had years to talk but never did. Why now? What changed?

The room suddenly became still. He could hear the now steady beep of the heart monitor. The doctor came over and spoke. "Your father seems to have suffered another heart attack. We will monitor him closely."

"Is he conscious?"

"Sorry, but we needed to put him into a medically induced coma so his body can try to heal. We have yet to determine what continues to cause his heart rate to increase and blood pressure to soar. It's as though there is an internal battle happening that we cannot see."

Brice nodded. He understood that feeling. It was what he'd been going through himself. He wondered if his father was considering all the feelings he never shared and was now reliving them in his head.

"We'll monitor him closely."

"Thank you."

Brice looked at his watch. Dean should've been here almost two hours ago. No matter how badly he wanted to go home, especially with Lena there waiting for him, he couldn't. He would stay, even if it meant waiting until morning when Alexander came.

As he was trying to make himself comfortable in the chair, a nurse came in with a blanket and pillow. "I thought you might want to use these."

Too tired to respond, he took them and leaned back. Twenty-four hours ago he demanded Lena come with him to his home where he could protect her. What did he do? He left her there, alone with the staff. Yes, she was safe, protected by hired men, but not him. That was not how he had envisioned the night to go.

He hadn't been able to stop thinking about her since they had wild sex in his office. She'd rekindled a fire that couldn't be extinguished. Everything within him wanted to be with her in his bed, making love to her all night long until she couldn't remember her name.

But he couldn't be any farther away from where he wanted to be. *So why am I still here?* He looked at his father one last time before drifting off to sleep. *A father was meant to protect his children, not berate and belittle them. But he hadn't kicked us out of our home. We may not have felt love from him, but he provided for us. Why am I still here? Because if I had a son, I would want him with me.*

Chapter Sixteen

I T WAS ANOTHER long night, and his body ached from what little sleep he did get on that hard plastic chair. *I need to make a donation to this unit.* As a chemical engineer, he had studied with many people in the medical field, yet he couldn't ever remember a time where he actually visited anyone in the hospital. It hadn't seemed odd to him until now. How was it a thirty-eight-year-old man had been able to avoid that?

It wasn't that no one had been sick or injured, but when something did happen, his father had the doctors come to the house; even X-ray machines could be mobile. *We've been lucky no one has needed surgery.* He wasn't sure if it was a perk of growing up with money or just another level of control his father wouldn't relinquish. *What did all this get you, Dad? You're in the hospital in a coma. Where's all your control now?*

Last night was like a slap in the face. You couldn't ask for a better reality check than watching someone on the verge of losing their life's battle.

His father had worked hard building his business.

And he'd been damn successful at it. Even now Brice wouldn't want to go head to head with his father if there were a company he had set his eyes on. There was nothing that would stop him from getting what he wanted. The price was never too high nor the risk too great.

Brice thought of the project they were now in the middle of. Trundaie was where they wanted to be. Even with all the signs beforehand warning them this might not be a wise choice, they'd forged forward. *The difference, Dad, is we know when to back off. Sometimes the prize is not worth the price.*

For Brice the price was family. He had nothing that resembled anything like his friends' families. The Barringtons gathered for family times and even let his siblings join in. *Not that Dad knew we went. He would have laid into our asses if he ever found out.* Over the years, they all had mastered lying. Not something to be proud of, but a talent needed if they ever wanted to see anything outside of their home. *The only time we all sat down together was when Dad introduced us to the latest nanny and reviewed the rules and restrictions. No one ever listened. They meant nothing to us as we all knew we were going to break them anyway. Some more than others.*

No matter how much they rebelled or caused trouble, their father only acted as the disciplinarian, never the comforter. Maybe it was because they had no mother and he thought coddling would make his sons weak, but understanding or encouragement would have been nice.

Unfortunately, he was very much his father's son. He was demanding and only accepted the results he asked for, anything less cost his employees their job. He believed in second chances, just not at his company. Brice still considered himself a shrewd businessman, one with a conscience but not necessarily a heart.

Finally back home, standing in his foyer, he arched his back and cracked his neck. The sunrise was only an hour away, and the weekend was about to begin. He couldn't remember the last time he hadn't spent it at the office. With the formula on hold, pending the resolution regarding plant location, he could do nothing but wait. He had all the time he wanted to do anything he chose. What exactly that was going to be he didn't know. He did know a woman was at his house who wasn't too happy with him the last time he saw her. He knew how he would like to spend the day, but he wasn't so sure she would share the same thoughts. *But I can be damn persuasive when I want to be.*

LENA COULDN'T SLEEP. No calls from Brice at all. She knew he had a lot on his mind, but what about her? Didn't all this craziness affect her as well? He'd pulled her from her apartment, and now she was trapped in his house. *What am I complaining about? I feel safer here than I did in my apartment, but for someone who is never alone, never idle, this is not me. Luxury. This isn't permanent, Lena, so don't get used to it. God, I must be losing my mind.*

Standing in her T-shirt and socks, she flipped the

bacon. It had taken her almost an hour to find the hidden utensils. The kitchen was the size of most people's apartments. If he didn't have it, then it probably didn't exist. *With all this stuff, he must do a lot of entertaining.*

Her mind wondered who he might entertain. Did he bring women here? Had he used this kitchen with them? Had they gotten distracted and made love on the marble center island?

She was jealous, but why? They weren't together, and he was a strong, virile, healthy man. *With a robust sexual appetite.* Did she think he'd abstained since he left her? No, that was impossible. She may not have been with anyone after him, but her circumstances were different. She had a son. *Well, so does he, but he doesn't know that yet.*

If she hadn't been pregnant, would she have moved on, found someone else? *Where would I be now without Nicholas?* The thought of not having him in her life brought her to tears. Although it had been far from easy, she wouldn't have changed a thing. He brought her all the joy in the world. He was a sweet-spirited boy like her and highly intelligent like his father. There wasn't a time when she gave him a new toy that he didn't try to figure out what made it work. He had to take everything apart. *God help me when he finds out what a screwdriver can do. He'll probably take apart the entire house.* Looking around the kitchen, she laughed. Maybe I just need a bigger house to keep him occupied.

With her breakfast made, she went to pour herself a second cup of coffee.

"Did you make enough for two?"

Startled by the sound of his voice, she knocked her cup over, causing it to splash some of the hot coffee down the front of her T-shirt. Instinctively she pulled it off her so she wouldn't get burned. With a sigh of relief, she held it to her bare chest before turning to face him.

"Don't you know better than to sneak up on people? God, you scared me half to death." Her voice was filled with adrenaline from the near accident.

His eyes roamed over her. Although her private parts were covered, she was far from decent. The hunger in his eyes was hotter than the coffee, and her flesh became alive with need. *Don't look at me like that, Brice. I can't. We can't. Not again.*

The kitchen that had seemed massive was closing in on her now. She needed to get out of there before she became lost in her own desires. "Excuse me." She moved to the left and tried to make it out of the room, but he caught the edge of the T-shirt and tugged it free from her grasp. Stopping dead in her tracks, she crossed her arms and cupped her bare breasts. Running wouldn't discourage him. He would only follow, and this was his house. There really wasn't any place to hide, not that she wanted to. She had been haunted by the memories of his touch. He wasn't her first, but he was her last. After being with him, she'd had no desire to be with anyone else. No one had ever made her feel as he did. *Not that I had the time or inclination to search for anyone really.* Whether he was a master at lovemaking or lovemaking was enhanced by her feelings for him, he brought her to heights she'd never experienced with anyone else. Her body ached to feel that again. No matter how wrong it was, she wanted him desperately.

Standing only in her pink satin panties and socks, she turned. *This is a bad idea.* Once her eyes met his, she was lost. He still held her T-shirt in his hand. Walking over to him she said, "I believe that belongs to me." Slowly she dropped her hands from her breasts. "Would you give it to me, please?"

His light gray eyes went dark. She knew he interpreted her seductive offer exactly how she meant it. Stepping only inches away, she let the tip of her tongue lick her lips, never looking away from his gaze.

A soft growl escaped him before he pulled her against him and claimed her lips. His kiss was hard and demanding. She opened to him willingly, giving him all she had to offer. Their tongues searched each other hungrily. She fought for control; he took it from her.

Lena melted into his embrace, wanting to feel more of him. Tugging at his shirt, she pulled it from his pants and began unbuttoning it. Brice removed his tie then threw it to the side. Their need for each other grew faster than he could remove his clothes.

He pulled away, gasping for air. Brice swooped her into his arms. "This time we're doing it right."

She didn't have any complaints about last time but

had to agree she wanted more this morning. She wanted everything he was willing to give her, and in turn, she was going to meet his every request. Lena wrapped her arms around his neck and nestled her head on his broad shoulders as he carried her to his bedroom.

Once inside he laid her on the bed and removed his remaining clothes. He didn't come right to her. Instead he stood at the foot of the bed, devouring her with his eyes. As his eyes made their way down her face, to her breast, then lower, she became self-conscious of her appearance. *I know, I've gained weight; I don't have the perfect body I had before.* She once had a toned, lean body, but after giving birth to their son, it was now softened with full curves. *Oh no, we can't do this. Not yet. I have to tell him about Nicholas first.*

"God, you're more beautiful than I remember." His voice was husky with need.

She reached for the blanket to cover herself. This couldn't continue. The truth had to be spoken now, before they made love. "Brice, I have to tell you something."

"I know. I feel it too. A connection like we had before."

Yes, that too. "Brice I need to tell you about—"

He bent down and claimed her lips before she could continue. Brice murmured against them, "This moment is about you and me." His lips trailed along her jaw and down her throat. "We'll talk later, but right now, I want to kiss all of your luscious body." His tongue darted out and licked the edge of her earlobe before biting it gently.

A moan escaped her lips as she arched against him. Was he right? Could what she had to say wait until later?

His mouth traveled down her neck and over her breast. "Please." She pleaded for his lips to take her.

Brice met her gaze before taking her taut nipple into his mouth. A rush of heat ran through her veins as he nipped and sucked her. His hand moved up her thigh, resting on her panties. Without missing a beat, he slid his hands around her backside and slipped them downward.

Lifting her hips off the bed, she helped him move lower. She didn't want anything between them. Once free, Brice moved his hands back up, this time his fingers slid between her folds. A shiver of pleasure rocked her. "You are so wet for me already."

Lena could feel the heat from his hard shaft against her legs. She opened for him, desperate to feel him inside her. He didn't enter her. Instead, he slowly brushed his fingers over her swollen clit. Her eyes closed as she wiggled herself closer to him, coaxing him to give more. He ignored her request and continued his slow assault on her. Each stroke sending pulsating signals to every nerve in her body.

You're killing me. Lena reached her hands up to pull him to her, but he grabbed her wrists and held them firmly above her head on the bed.

"Not until I make you purr."

Purr? Scream is more like it. He was driving her crazy, holding her body on the brink of release, yet not letting her go. "Please, I need you. I can't wait any longer."

As to ease the sweet torture, he slid one finger inside her and continued circling her clit. His strokes became faster, harder, then he added a second finger. She opened her legs farther so he could go deeper. Tossing her head from side to side, she struggled to free her hands, but he only tightened his grip. When she couldn't think any longer, her body began to shake as she clenched around his fingers. "Yes. Yes. Oh, God. Brice." Her climax continued wave after wave, and her screams of passion echoed throughout the room.

Before her senses came back, Brice was between her legs, removing his hand and replacing it with his large shaft. He didn't enter. Instead he teased her. Rubbing himself over her clit, between her folds, and back up again. Finally he stopped at her entrance. "Open your eyes and look at me." Her lids still heavy with desire fought to open. "Look at me, Lena. I want to see your eyes when I make love to you."

She did as he asked. As their eyes met she saw the raw passion within him. His need was great, and she knew he couldn't wait any longer. "I'm yours, Brice," she said breathlessly.

In one quick thrust his shaft filled her, and she gasped as the brief pain turned into sweet pleasure. He waited for her to become accustomed to him before moving. Her body clenched around him. He groaned in pleasure. "Yes, Lena, take all of me." He entered further.

Lena began rocking her hips. He moved to meet her.

He let go of her hands and grabbed her hips, pulling her up to meet him faster and harder. *I've missed you so much. I've needed this so badly.* "That feels so good."

"Baby, I'm going make you lose your mind." He plunged into her again and again. Her body was on fire. She was gasping for air, clawing at the sheets. Her body was begging to release, yet not wanting it to end. "Now, baby. Give it to me now."

His words ripped through her last restraint. Her climax was stronger than she had experienced before and rocked her again and again. A high-pitched scream escaped her lips and was met by a deep animalistic growl. Both of them tensed before he finally collapsed on top of her.

She could feel his heart pounding against her chest as he lay still. *This feels like heaven.* She wrapped her arms around him, kissed his shoulder, and heard him sigh softly before he rolled off her. Although he was much heavier than she was, she missed the weight of him instantly.

Now lying on his back, he reached around her and pulled her to rest on him. "Now my sweet angel, I need some sleep, then maybe breakfast."

It wasn't long before she heard his breathing relax and he was out cold. *Sleep now, but I haven't forgotten, we still need to talk.* Tightening her hold on him, she too began to doze. *I better enjoy this now because it's probably the last time you'll ever want to hold me.*

Chapter Seventeen

LENA HAD SLIPPED away while Brice continued to sleep. *Whatever you've been doing while out of the office, it seems to be stressing you more than usual.* She had decided that today was the big day. Time to come clean about what happened three years ago. Exactly how she was going to start that conversation wasn't clear. The only thing she knew was it had to be done. The more time that passed, the more difficult it was becoming. *The more I care what his reaction is going to be.* Caring meant he had somehow made his way back into her heart. She tried telling herself it was only because she had been sexually frustrated, and it was only his touch she missed. That was far from the truth. When he took her to what had been her favorite restaurant and remembered what she liked to eat, it spoke volumes. All this time she had thought he had forgotten her, yet he seemed to remember everything about her. *Except how to pick up a damn phone and call me.*

Neither of them needed to have gone through this alone. She would have supported his decision to leave his father's company and start his own business. Had he thought she would tell him he was crazy to walk away from such a successful business? Did he think she wouldn't stay with him while he struggled to get it going? *We could've struggled together instead of apart.*

Thinking about what could've been was a bad way to start the day. There was nothing she could do to change what happened. He didn't call her, and she had made the conscious decision not to make the first move either. *God, we're both so stubborn. Maybe we both made the right choice for where we were back then. Have we changed now though? If anything, he is a harder man than before.*

Was it possible he also was questioning his choice? Did he at least regret the harsh breakup? Had he been as tormented by his words as she had been? Part of her hoped so. No one should speak to someone they supposedly cared about in that manner. *Maybe that's what is stressing him out. His guilt. But that doesn't explain his cold contempt when he first saw me outside his office.*

You never really could run away from it. It was always part of you whether you acknowledged it or not. You did have options of what to do with it. Either live with it and have no future, or take what you have learned, apply what you can, so tomorrow you don't make those same mistakes.

Could it be more than what was transpiring between them that was causing his tension? Then she remembered he had a guard placed at her apartment. He knew where she lived. *What else does he know? Has he already figured out he is a father? Is that why he's demanding I come and stay with him? Is it all a lie about some huge threat from Trundaie? Can he be that controlling? Can he be that manipulative?*

Nothing at this point would surprise her. But if he knew, then why hadn't he asked to see Nicholas? *Maybe he's sending someone there now.* Uncontrollable panic filled her. Losing her son would kill her. *He won't do that to me. He can't.*

Grabbing her cell phone, she stepped outside and dialed her mother.

"Hi, Mom. I'm just checking in." Lena tried to cover her anxiety but knew her voice still trembled as she spoke.

"Hi, Lena. Your brother Gary is here playing with Nicholas. Can you believe he bought him a fishing pole and a book on different types of fish? I told Gary that Nicholas wasn't going to able to use that when he goes back to Boston, but Gary insisted he could use it when you come for visits on the weekends."

He's there. Safe and happy. Why had she thought any differently? Her parents would never let anyone take her child. *Not even someone as rich and powerful as Brice Henderson.* One thing she knew was once a Razzi, always a Razzi. No one was going to change that. Family was everything to them. Of course, that was why it hurt her parents so much when she didn't live close by. "I'll make sure he gets to use that fishing pole as often as we can, as long as Uncle Gary is willing to teach him." She was pleased her family's early morning fishing adventures with the guys were going to be passed down to the next generation. *I don't know if you're into fishing, Nicholas, but you're going to have to learn how to fake it. Just like I did.*

It felt good knowing at least one of her brothers had taken some serious interest in her son. The first few times Gary had seen him, he didn't even want to hold him. "I don't do babies," he had said. She didn't blame him. They were delicate and needy beings, and her brother had been worried he would drop him. It was funny to watch. A roofer by trade, he didn't have a fear of heights, but a little seven-pound baby shook him to the core. He said his rough hands would probably scare the baby, but she knew it was more than that. Even then he'd loved his little nephew and had feared he would do the wrong thing.

Lena was very familiar with that feeling. Every night a parent questions the day, and then in the morning starts it all over again. *How did you handle it all without driving yourself crazy with worry, Mom? It seems that's all I do.*

Confident everything was safe back home, she could relax. After she showered and dressed, she quickly found herself bored. Having nothing to do became old quick. She was used to a routine, one she enjoyed. Sitting alone twiddling her thumbs didn't suit her at all.

With the house still quiet, she went to the kitchen where her uneaten breakfast waited. Wasting food wasn't something she normally did, but hours had passed, and there was only one place for her breakfast now. *The trash.*

She finished washing the dishes from her uneaten breakfast and debated if a second attempt was in order. He had promised her breakfast, yet it was already past noon.

Leaning with her back against the sink, she wasn't caught off guard when Brice came around the corner. He walked over and kissed her lightly. "Good morning."

Smiling she replied, "Good afternoon."

"Guess I was more tired than I thought. Have you eaten yet?"

That's what I was trying to do when you came home this morning. Not complaining, though. "I thought I would wait for you."

"Do you remember that little diner we used to go to that served breakfast all day?"

The one we used to go to every Saturday morning after making love all Friday night? Yeah, how could I forget? "I think so, but I thought we were going to talk."

"Not on an empty stomach." He pulled her into his arms. Grabbing her by the ass, he jacked her up against him and kissed her firmly. "It's been a long time since I had a weekend off. Let's enjoy it."

It sounded wonderful to her. A weekend like they used to share, but it wasn't real. None of this was. Once she told him about Nicholas, it was all going to change. "Brice, there is something I need to tell you."

"Later. I promise, I will listen to anything you feel

you need to say, but not at this moment."

Okay, Brice. I will do it your way. But just remember, I wanted to tell you, you just wouldn't listen. Just like three years ago. Warning bells echoed through her. *That doesn't bring me comfort. In fact, it makes me feel worse.*

HAVING HER HERE all weekend was good. *Too good.* It reminded him of how things could've been had they stayed together. Life would be so different than it was now. *Who knows, maybe I would even have a family of my own.*

It didn't look like any of the Henderson clan was headed in that direction. Five boys and one girl, all of them incapable of a serious relationship. *Thanks, Dad. You fucked up every single one of us.*

He found Lena sitting on the couch with her feet up, totally absorbed in the book she was reading. Brice didn't want to disturb her, but it was his shift at the hospital, and he didn't want to just disappear on her. Especially considering how comfortable she finally was around him.

Brice lifted her feet, sat on the couch, and rested her legs across his lap. "What are you reading?" A hint of pink came across her cheeks. "Hmm, that good huh? Want to read it to me?" He enjoyed teasing her but wouldn't have minded one bit if she read to him.

She put the book down. "Are you going somewhere?"

He nodded. It was time for the talk. *Or at least the beginning of one.* "Yeah. Do you remember Zoey calling?"

"She called you a few times. Do you mean the one

time you actually took the call?"

Don't miss much, do you? "Yes that time, smart ass." He laughed. "She told me my father was in the hospital and not doing well."

Lena sat up, touched his shoulder, and said, "I'm sorry to hear that. Has he been sick long?"

How much should he tell her? Opening up wasn't something he liked to do. He wanted a new beginning with her and the only way to do so was to try to be as they were before. Brice wasn't positive what the result for such honesty was, and he wasn't sure he knew what the truth was.

"Lena, you know I wasn't close to my father when you and I were dating. He is a difficult person to be around. Always has been."

"Everyone's family has issues."

This is beyond most. I would call it child abuse. "True. But there were reasons why I didn't take you to my family's home often. I didn't want you exposed to that type of treatment."

"He was . . . outspoken."

Brice laughed. "You just can't be mean, can you? That's one thing I've always loved about you. No matter how fucked up someone was, you still wouldn't call them out on it." *Unlike me.* "I have no problem telling you my father has always been a complete asshole."

"Brice, you shouldn't say that. I'm sure he tried his best."

Shaking his head, he replied, "He tried to do only

one thing: Make us all miserable. For the most part, he succeeded."

"I only know you and Zoey, but you both seem to have turned out okay. He must have done something right."

Was she correct? Did he blame his father for everything or were some things his fault? He had been searching for those answers ever since he saw his father in the hospital for the first time two weeks ago. Even now he didn't know. He had six children for some reason. *At some point, he must have loved us. Wanted us.*

"We turned out better than him so maybe you're right." *I can't think of anything, but there must be something.* "So the night I didn't come home I was sitting with my father. He's in a coma, and we're not sure if he is going to pull through." He watched her eyes glisten on the verge of tears. He knew his father had been far from kind to her, yet she was a sensitive soul and obviously she didn't want to see anyone suffer, even someone who had been unkind to her. *You're such a better person than me, Lena. Always have been and probably always will be.*

"Think positive, Brice."

"I'm not telling you this because I want your sympathy. It has brought up a lot of old feelings and issues. Things I hadn't thought about since I was a teenager, and honestly, I prefer it to stay that way. Unfortunately, sitting in a hospital room with no one to talk to leaves a lot of time to think, to dwell on things you normally wouldn't."

"That can be a good thing sometimes."

"Some of it was. It made me think of things I want to be different in my life." *I might not be able to change everything, but I refuse to be him.* "That's where I'm heading now. We're taking shifts, and mine is tonight."

"Would you like me to go with you, so you don't have to sit alone?"

You're an amazing woman, Lena. I'm not sure I would offer to do the same. "Thanks, but you don't want to spend the night there, trust me. I don't even want to be there."

"You don't have to be alone, and it would give us a chance to talk."

Leaning over, he kissed her on the forehead. "Sleep tonight. After work tomorrow, we can go to dinner and talk then."

He could tell she wanted to argue with him, but he didn't want to hear it. This weekend had been nearly perfect, and he wanted to keep it that way. Whatever she needed to tell him could wait. *Twenty-four hours won't make that much difference.*

Chapter Eighteen

"BENNETT, YOU BETTER be calling with some good news regarding Trundaie." Brice didn't know this guy, but with his recommendations, it was wise to heed his warnings.

"Things are stable . . . well, as stable as they get in that country. Asher's brother Ian played an important part with some diplomatic negotiations. He's one fucking genius when it comes to diplomacy. You would never know those two are brothers."

Glad to see you took my advice, Asher. Bennett was right. Asher was so unlike Ian or any other member of his family. Diplomacy was a term he probably didn't have in his vocabulary. *Not that I do either.* "Any news about the plant?"

"Looks as though that option is still available for B&H. Now it's up to you and Asher to decide if you want to proceed."

He was relieved to hear things could go back to normal. Lena would be able to go back to her apartment. *When I decide to pass along the message. I'm not in any rush to let you go, Lena.*

Brice's night hadn't been filled with thoughts of his childhood as it had been the night before. This time, all he could think of was Lena and how fucking sexy she was. She'd always been gorgeous, but she'd become more so over the years. Was that because he'd missed her or because he felt so connected to her? He would be lying if he said he hadn't given her any thought over the last three years. What they had shared before was something he hadn't ever shared with another person. Letting her go hadn't been easy, for her or him. *Had I loved her back then? Is that why I've never been able to forget her? I'm not sure I know what love is. Or if I'm even capable of it.*

He would need to figure out what he wanted soon. Her assignment was coming to an end, and Nancy had advised him she'd be back next Monday. *Thankfully her mother was recovering well. Unfortunately, that meant no excuse for Lena to stay. Lena. Is that what I want now? Do I want her to stay in my life this time? Will she want to? She told me she was mine last night, but was that only in a moment of passion?*

His thoughts were cut off when his replacement entered the hospital room. "You look like you're in deep thought. Something troubling you, Brice?"

"Good morning, Zoey. No changes with Dad."

"Ignoring my questions? Hmm, let me imagine what could be troubling you."

He was not in the mood for her games today. *Actually never will be. Someday she will get that.* "I've got to get to work."

Zoey stood in the doorway, blocking his exit. "If it's not Dad, then what is it? You mentioned issues with work. Did you get those resolved?"

"Work is fine, Dad is fine, everything is great." *Now stop with the questions already.*

She eyed him as she always did. He knew she didn't believe him, but he didn't care. It was the only answer she was getting from him.

"So how is your temporary assistant working out?" When he went to answer, she raised her hand. "I know. Great. Did you know we went to lunch together the day you blew me off?"

No, he didn't. Zoey must have made Lena very uncomfortable with her list of questions or stories about the good ole days. *No wonder Lena acted differently. Knowing Zoey, she must have said something to Lena innocently that rekindled the pain he had put her through.*

"She's really changed. I'd thought you were going to ask her to marry you and give me a nephew and niece."

"Let's not take a trip down Memory Lane."

"Funny, she didn't seem to want to either. But I can understand her. I mean she obviously has someone special in her life now."

She talked about Rex? Bennett said he was nothing to her. Was he wrong? "We don't discuss our personal lives at work, Zoey."

"Too bad. She is such a sweet woman, and I bet she is a wonderful mother, too."

Mother? "Lena doesn't have any children."

A look of surprise came over her face. "Boy, brother dear, you weren't kidding when you said you don't talk about anything personal. Yes, she has a child. A son."

She's got to be wrong. Lena's been with me for a few days, and I didn't see a child when I picked her up. She hasn't mentioned a child, so there can't be one. Whatever Zoey thought she knew she was way off the mark.

"Zoey, like I said before, I have things I need to attend to. Why don't you stay here and try to keep out of trouble?"

MONDAYS NORMALLY DRAGGED, and she dreaded them. Today had flown by. Maybe it was because it was her last week, or it could be she was still flying high from the weekend with Brice. Either way this day was nearly perfect. Only having Nicholas home with her would make it absolutely perfect.

When she called her mother earlier to let her know she would be down Friday night for Nicholas, she heard her mother's sadness. "Maybe you can spend the weekend with us before heading back." Lena didn't make any promises, but there was no reason to rush back. There wasn't a job waiting for her yet, but she knew Talent Hunters had lined something up for the end of April. Even though she and Brice were getting along better than she ever dreamed they would, she knew it wasn't going to last. *Not after I tell him about Nicholas.*

He had rejected me, so he doesn't really have any cause

to be angry at my decision. He had made it clear he wasn't interested in family, and despite how easy it had been with him these last two days, she didn't think his feelings on the matter had actually changed. From what she had heard from his siblings, things were heading in the opposite direction. *He had said we would talk, but do I bring it up tonight? Perhaps I should wait until Friday when I will be leaving him anyway. Leaving him . . . again, and forever this time. It has to be said. No matter the price. It has to be done.* She could only imagine his reaction. He probably was going to think she took the temp job just to weasel her way back into his life so she could drop the news on him. Lena wasn't calculating by any means. Hopefully, she would be able to make him see this was all coincidence, nothing more. *Except for the one white lie. Nicholas.*

Funny, because she was one who never lied, so when she did, she went big. *At least by Friday it will be all over. No more hiding. I'll have my answer, and he'll have a son.*

When she thought about it, it seemed like it should be simple. But nothing in life ever was, and this was as complex as it could get.

As Brice had promised, he took her to dinner. This time, she wasn't uptight or forced to go. It was a perfect night for a date. The weather had warmed enough for a stroll after dinner before heading back to his house.

Once inside, they sat in front of the fireplace and chatted like an ordinary couple about their day.

"Any news about the threats?"

He shrugged his shoulders. "It's safer for you at my house."

That wasn't much of an answer, but she understood he didn't want to worry her. It was nice being taken care of, even if it wasn't going to be forever. "Oh, I forgot to tell you. A sweet woman called today to invite you to an art auction. Some woman, Emily Harris from New England, is going to be showing her mother's artwork. I found it so interesting."

"Why is that?" Brice asked while rubbing Lena's shoulders.

"The woman who created the artwork was blind. Imagine that. And Emily wants to create a museum to display works of art that the blind can go and see. Well, not see, but feel I guess. I know it sounds crazy to think of a museum for the blind, but from what she was telling me, it sounded amazing. I really think you should go."

"To a museum for the blind?"

Lena laughed. "No. To the auction that is displaying the artwork."

"Lena, I don't take sales calls and don't go to invites when people decide to call me out of the blue. I'm a busy man, and if I said yes to everything, I wouldn't ever get my work done."

"Funny. She said you would probably say that. I was to remind you that you have not been around in a long time. The entire family will be there, and she was expecting to see you. And not just you. The invitation was for all the Hendersons."

"Who are you talking about?"

"Sophie Barrington, Asher's mother. She sounded like such sweet woman. Once she got talking I couldn't get her to stop. But then again, I was enjoying hearing all about it anyway. She even talked about you when you used to play at her house. I can't picture what you were like as a child. I asked her, but she said it would be better if I heard it from you."

"Mrs. Barrington. It has been a long time since I've seen her. When did she say this event was taking place?"

Lena was pleased she had piqued his interest. It was not only a worthy cause, but it would do him good to go out and mingle with people away from work. "She said you should remember because you used to attend each year."

He looked puzzled.

Shaking her head she gave him what he asked for. "In two weeks she will host the art auction. It's always the second week of April for some reason. I asked, but she wouldn't say why. She said all proceeds this year will support the St. Jude Children's Hospital. I think it's something you should go to."

He arched a brow and said, "There are a lot of things I should do Lena. I choose not to."

She didn't want to admit it, but something deep inside her wanted him to ask her to go to the auction. She would have accepted too, even though it would not have been a wise choice. Not with the way things were between them right now. The auction sounded amazing and Lena wanted to be there, but that was nothing compared to the longing within her to know he still cared. *Why, Lena? Why are you accepting his scraps of attention? He isn't looking for someone for forever, but rather a possession. One he will throw away when he tires of it. You aren't happy being his sexual plaything, yet here you are, wishing he will ask, so you have an excuse to be with him again.* Her own thoughts pained her. She knew she needed to think this through, to understand her own desires, and to feel wanted by him, even if only temporarily.

Apparently he didn't notice her disappointment. *Why should he? He's probably used to disappointing people all the time. Why should I be any different?*

"Sounds like you had an interesting day today. I chatted briefly with my sister while I was sitting with my father."

"That's great. I knew you didn't really want to be alone. I'm glad you had someone with you. How is she doing through all this?" Lena knew it was difficult on Brice even if he didn't want to admit it. Women were more sensitive to these things, so it must have been terrible for Zoey. She should reach out and ask her to lunch. She hadn't been kind to Zoey the last time they met. But then again she hadn't known about their father at that time.

"She was her usual self. Full of questions and full of stories."

"Zoey misses you, Brice. When we went to lunch,

she talked about how little she sees of you. How you lock yourself away in your lab and shut out the entire world. Is that true?"

He was quiet for a moment. "Yes, it is. I've changed."

"I see that, but I also see the person you were is still in there. What happened? I mean we never spoke about what occurred but obviously something did."

"Lena, Zoey likes to talk. That's all. You can't take everything she says seriously. You should hear some of the things she believes."

"It can't be all that bad. She seems very normal to me."

"Really? I doubt you'll think so after I tell you this."

Sitting back she crossed her arms in front of her. "Did she tell you a scary bedtime story?"

Laughing he said, "Something like that. Really a nightmare for us both."

"What does that mean?"

"That you are unobtainable."

Now you really have me puzzled. "Are you talking in riddles because I have no idea what you're talking about?"

"Of course you don't because it's not true."

"What isn't?"

"That you are seeing someone and that you're a mommy to a baby boy."

His laughter echoed through her, and she stood up quickly. Her heart was pounding. *He knows, yet he doesn't. Oh God, help me.* Her worse nightmare had come true. He knew and wouldn't accept it. *You don't want Nicholas.* The shock was too great. The room began to spin, and then everything went black.

Chapter Nineteen

*O*H GOD, LENA. He sprang from his seat and caught her in his arms before she hit the floor. He laid her on the couch and tapped her cheek lightly. "Lena." She stirred and moaned softly. "Wake up, Lena."

Slowly her eyes fluttered opened. "What . . . what happened?" Her voice was barely a whisper.

He was filled with relief, hearing her voice. He had never experienced such fear in his life. Everything was great, they were joking around and then boom, down she went. There hadn't been any advanced warning. If he hadn't been there she would have hit the floor. "You fainted." Brice bent over and kissed her forehead. "You're okay. I caught you."

Lena tried to sit up, but he held her so she couldn't move. She was still pale, and he had yet to figure out what caused her to faint in the first place.

"You're not going anywhere until I know you are okay." He did the only thing he knew to do, felt her forehead for a fever. She didn't feel overly warm to him, but he was no expert. "Tell me how you're feeling now.

Does anything hurt? Your head or anything else?"

She shook her head. "A bit dizzy, that's all. I'm sure if I lie down for a minute I'll be okay."

"God, baby, you scared the hell out of me." As someone always in control, feeling helpless had not been good. "I think we should go to the hospital. Let them check you out to make sure everything is okay."

"I'm okay. It was just a—"

Just what? Tell me what's going on? "Lena, if you know what happened, tell me."

She closed her eyes and answered. "Just stress."

"Talk to me, Lena. What's bothering you? Let me help you."

"I do want to . . . need to talk to you about something. Something I have been trying to talk to you about for a while."

He knew she had wanted to talk. He had put her off several times because he didn't want to hear about Rex. Was it something more than that? Did she need his help all this time, and he had left her to handle it alone? "I'm sorry, I should have listened before now." Brice brushed a stray strand of her wild black curly hair away from her face. "Let's get you settled first, then we can talk when you're feeling up to it. And this time, I won't interrupt you."

Lena nodded. "I'm ready now if you are."

ALTHOUGH HER HEAD still had a dull ache, she knew it was nothing compared to what Brice was about to feel.

She had never fainted before, but the shock of what he had said about her having a baby must have been too much with the other stress she had been facing lately.

This is not how she envisioned starting the conversation, but at least it was going to take place. *Way overdue.*

"Brice, I think you should sit down." Lena moved her legs off the couch and sat up. "This isn't going to be a quick conversation, and I'm sure you will have your share of questions after. And I'll answer whatever questions you have."

He looked at puzzled but did as she asked. Once seated near her he took her hand in his. "Okay. I'm listening."

He held her hand, and she felt the togetherness she had been longing for. He truly was there for her, but would he be after? Was what she was about to tell him going to end what future they may have had? *Do I want a future with him?*

It doesn't matter. Brice needs to know about Nicholas, and I hope he is more receptive to being a father than he lets on. There was only one way to find out.

"Do you remember the night we broke up?" *Ease him in. No reason to send him into shock too.*

"It wasn't my finest moment. There was a lot going on at that time, and I made a choice that I know hurt you. I want to be honest with you, though, I'm not sure if given the chance, I'd do things differently. I did what I felt I needed to do at that time."

She wasn't trying to make him feel guilty about their

breakup, she only wanted him to recall that time. The fact that even now he would still do it all over again didn't make this any easier. Was he better off not knowing about Nicholas? *Does he deserve to know?*

"But that was a long time ago, Lena. I'm not the same person I was then."

That was true. But in many ways it wasn't a good thing. The person he was before was someone she could picture playing with Nicholas in the park. The man sitting next to her, holding her hand, she wasn't so sure.

The last three weeks had brought them almost full circle to where they were right before they broke up. Was this about to be an instant replay? Would he decide again his work was the only important thing in his life? *I can protect my heart, but how do I protect Nicholas's?*

"Neither of us are, Brice. I have changed as well. But this isn't about our breakup. It's about so much more." Although she needed his support and strength, Lena pulled her hand free of his. "Back then we were supposed to go out for a celebration dinner. I had told you there was something we needed to discuss, and you said we would talk about it over dinner. If you remember, that dinner didn't happen. So I tried to talk to you at my apartment, but you weren't in the mood to hear it then either."

Her heart was pounding. This was more difficult than anyone could imagine. It would be so much easier if she didn't care so damn much about him. Then his feelings and his anger would not affect her in any way.

"At that time no one could talk to me. I was furious with my father and had only one thing on my mind. I wanted to show him I didn't need a father and that I was capable of being more without him than with him. All I wanted to do was distance myself from him in every way possible. You don't know what it was like growing up in a house with a father who would never love you. At that time I wanted to be anything but his son."

She could see the pain from that time hadn't totally dissipated. Any other time and she would have reached out to him to comfort him, to let him know what a wonderful man he had turned out to be despite who his father was. That conversation would take place, but not now.

"You did what you needed to do at that time. I made choices then too. It wasn't easy and I'm not even sure if it was the correct one, but there is no going back and changing either of ours now. All we can do is move forward."

"I thought you wanted to talk about the past. Are you saying that it's our future that is stressing you?"

Oh, how they blend together. Lena wasn't sure why she wanted him to understand what occurred back then. It didn't change anything now. Was she delaying the evitable on purpose? Could it be that she hoped the past would be the link needed to the future? *I'm not sure, so how can I ask him?* "I do. We can't change the past. Neither of us can. But sometimes your past has a way of creeping back in when you least expect it."

"Do you mean Rex?" Brice's voice was dry and cold.

Rex? God, no. What did he have to do with any of this? *Nothing.* Was Brice actually jealous of a man who was only a friend? *If it were only so simple.* "No. Rex is only a friend. Nothing more."

"Then what from our past do we need to bring into our future because I'm okay with leaving it there and moving on. In case you have forgotten, I'm not really a person who likes to share much. Digging up the past is something that would fall into that category."

Our past has destined our future. "It is what I have been trying to tell you, now and three years ago." Taking a deep breath to summon all her courage she turned to him and met his eyes so he could see her sincerity as she spoke. "You have a son."

It was his turn to look pale. The shock was evident and at first he had a look of disbelief. His light gray eyes turned almost black when she didn't turn away.

"I'm a father. Since when?" His tone was as sharp as she anticipated it would be.

"That night we broke up. That was the news I wanted to share with you." She paused momentarily. "This is what I have been trying to talk to you about."

Brice got up and began to pace. He ran his hands through his hair and looked like he wanted to punch something. She could only imagine what he must be thinking. All these years and all that lost time. He must hate her right now, and she couldn't blame him. She didn't particularly like herself at this moment.

When he turned to speak the words were not something she had prepared herself for. "You're not the woman I thought you were. The woman I loved never would have done this. I know you hated me, but why do that to him? If you didn't want him, then you should have come to me. I would've raised him without you."

Not want my son? What is he talking about? Nicholas is my life. "I love him more than you will ever understand. Everything I did was for his best interest, never my own."

Anger filled the room. "Is that why you gave him away? You thought I was going to be such a horrible father that you'd rather have some stranger raise him than me?"

"Brice, this had nothing to do with you."

"It has everything to do with me."

"I know. I mean my decision to not tell you. It wasn't about if I thought you would be a good father. It was . . . that I wasn't sure you wanted to be a father."

"So you took the choice away from me? You decided on your own what was best for my son?"

"Our son," she reminded him. "Yes, I made that choice. And I'm not sure I wouldn't make the same choice now." Throwing his own words back at him from earlier was mean and uncalled for, but so were his accusations.

He came to stand directly in front of her. "Do you know where he is now? How he is being treated? Is he okay? Happy?"

"Of course I do. What kind of mother do you think I

am?"

"One who gave our child away."

Away? He thinks I didn't keep him? "Brice. You are wrong. My son . . . our son is my entire world. I has never been a day I was without him until recently. And that is only because you said there was a threat and I couldn't risk him being hurt. I would die if anything happened to him."

He glared at her. His nostrils flared as he huffed in anger. "Where is he?"

Swallowing, she knew she would have to answer. He would go, and for better or worse, everyone would know her secret. *Nicholas's father is Brice Henderson.*

"What about the threat?"

"It's over."

And you failed to tell me? Why? So you can keep me here under your control? It didn't matter anymore. After this she was sure he would pack her bags and throw her out.

"He's at my parents' home in Plymouth. If you would like, we can go see him now."

Brice walked over to the counter, grabbed his cell phone and keys. "Take me to my son."

Chapter Twenty

I T WAS OVER. She'd told him. Lena turned to look at him. She couldn't read his expression, but could only imagine how he felt. In less than an hour he would be meeting his son for the first time. *This is a good thing. For both of them.* She wanted to call her parents, give them the heads-up, but in the heat of the moment she'd forgotten to take her phone with her. The last thing she wanted to do was ask him to use his phone. *Don't want to look any more irresponsible than you think I am already.*

That left only one option. Prepare him for what he was going to walk into. "Brice. I know you're angry."

"You think?"

"I would be too. But I need to ask a favor of you."

He turned to her. His eyes still dark. "Do you believe I owe you one?"

No, you don't. But I don't owe you anything either. "I'm not asking for me. This is for Nicholas and my parents."

"Ah, my son has a name. I was wondering if you were going to tell me or make me wait another three years to find out."

Ouch. You do know how to hurt me, don't you? "Brice, you can be angry with me all you want, I don't care. I stopped caring three years ago when you cut me out of your life and never looked back. We both made mistakes. At least I have admitted to mine. I really am sorry, and I know I could say it a million times over, but it won't change the past. We both fucked up back then but we don't have to continue on that path now. There are people who didn't do anything to you and don't even know you. They are innocent in this and don't deserve to experience your wrath."

"My wrath? Is that what you think this is? Trust me, Lena, if it was, you wouldn't be sitting next to me. My son would be with me and you would never see him again."

Panic filled her. Would he do such a thing? *Can he? Take Nicholas away from me*? She knew it was a possibility and with his money and power, it would be difficult to stop him, but he had to know what that would do to her. What she had done was horrible, but that was too great a punishment. "Please Brice, I—"

"I'm not going to take him away from you, Lena. But I will be a part of his life. A very big part, do you understand?"

I wouldn't want it any other way. It's what is best for Nicholas. What I always wanted. "I do. Brice, I haven't told anyone who his father is."

He arched a brow. "What do you mean? What did

you tell your parents? Do they think you had him on your own?"

Still trying to anger me? I'm not falling for it, Brice. I have too much to lose so I'll ignore you sharp words and keep the peace, for Nicholas. "No. They asked. Many times. But I refused to answer. You said that no one was more important to you than *your* future. I didn't want anyone trying to force you to see things differently. If my father had known who you were he would have insisted on sitting you down for a man-to-man talk. I didn't want you to want Nicholas out of guilt or obligation. I wanted you only to want him out of love."

"I'm not one who is easily intimidated, and trust me, no one could force me to do anything I didn't want to do. Not then and sure as hell not now."

They didn't speak the remainder of the ride. It was uncomfortable but as they pulled up to her parents' house, she knew it was going to get worse. *Great, my brothers are here too.*

THERE HAD BEEN so much to process on the way over. Lena may be the one who had fainted, but he was the one in shock. *I have a son.* The words replayed over and over again. He was far from happy that she had withheld the existence of Nicholas for over three years, but he knew he wasn't without blame. *I was a total fuck-up back then. It was all about me, and I didn't care who got hurt.*

Maybe Lena's choice had been the right one. Would he have only resented Nicholas then? Would he have felt as though she was only telling him to hold on to him? He'd been untrustworthy and very bitter. *I acted more like my father than I ever had before. I wouldn't want my son exposed to me like that either.*

Even on the way there, he was unsure if this was the correct move. Brice never reacted to anything. The only time he had was when he fought with his father. Now after Lena delivered her news, he once again was reacting, not thinking things through. He knew he needed to see Nicholas. He wanted to be part of his life. Would that be good for Nicholas? *If I am even half the person my father is, Lena should keep him away from me.*

Like Lena, he had no plans to mention anything about Nicholas to his family. It would only cause more issues. For now, this was going to have to stay between him and Lena.

The limo pulled up to the house. Lena turned to him and asked, "Are you ready?"

No. I'm not sure what I am. "Don't worry about it."

She went first, knocked on the door, then opened it. "Mom. Dad," she shouted, but no one answered. "Hello, anyone home?"

There had been cars in the driveway so the house shouldn't be vacant. "Is this your usual greeting?"

Lena turned and looked at him sharply. "No one was expecting me. I'm sure they are not far because it's almost Nicholas's bed time."

Right after she said it the door opened behind them.

"Mama. Mama," the little boy shouted again and

again as he ran into Lena's open arms.

Brice watched as she picked him up and kissed his cheeks and hugged him so tight that Brice thought she would break him.

"Oh, Nicholas. Mama has missed you so much. Do you know how much Mama loves you?"

Nicholas opened his arms as wide as they could go and laughed saying, "Dis much, Mama. Dis much."

Lena started the hugging and kissing all over again. He could do nothing but watch the tender interaction between them. Brice never doubted she'd be a good mother. She was a wonderful person so why wouldn't she pass that along to her child. *He* wasn't such a nice guy. What did he have to give? *Not the lessons my father taught me.*

"And who do we have here?"

"Oh, Mom, Dad, I would like to introduce you to Brice Henderson. He's—"

"A friend of Lena's." He wasn't ready to announce his paternity just yet. This child might be his son, but the reality of it all was just hitting him. Watching the bond between mother and child opened a wound of his own. He never had experienced it and wasn't sure if he was capable of the bonding required to be a good parent.

"Welcome. I'm Ernest Razzi, Lena's father, and this lovely lady is my wife, Mary."

Brice shook hands with them both. "And these fine gentlemen are Gary and Tyler, Lena's older brothers."

"Nice meeting you all."

"Lena. Why didn't you tell us you were coming? I thought we weren't going to see you until the weekend," Mary said.

"Sorry, Mom. Something came up and there was a change of plans. I should have called."

Mary laughed. "You never have to call. The door's always open for you and Nicholas. You know that."

"Yes, Mom, I do."

"Brice, why don't you come with us to the living room while those women sort out all their emotions? Hellos and goodbyes seem to take a long time in this house." Ernest pointed to a room on the right. He didn't want to sit with them. He was here for one reason only, to see Nicholas.

"We can't stay because we have a long ride back to Boston," Lena stated.

"Oh no you don't. You can't pop in like that and expect me to let you leave without even sitting down for a cup of tea." Mary grabbed Lena by the hand, dragging her off to what must be the kitchen.

"Well, son, looks like you have no choice but to sit with us now. Looks like my wife is about to give Lena the third degree." Ernest chuckled.

Brice glanced in the direction the women had gone.

Gary gave him a slap on the back. "Don't even think about going in there. My mother should work for the Secret Service. Once she gets you cornered, there's no escape. Trust me, follow my dad, much more relaxing."

When he entered the living room he found it comfortable, lived in. Unlike the formal rooms he grew up in, which had been furnished for appearance only, this room was one that had character and was obviously utilized. There was an overstuffed couch which he could picture Lena sitting on, eating popcorn with her school friends. On the far side of the room was a piano with sheet music, waiting for someone to play. All the Hendersons played. It had been a requirement of their father. He was so rebellious then and never appreciated the gift he had been given. He played now, but it never flowed from him. *I'm no musician. I wonder if Lena plays?* There was so much he didn't know about her. They had both chosen to keep their family lives separate when they'd dated earlier. He knew why he hid his, but why would she hide hers? They seemed acceptable. *Maybe it was me; maybe she didn't want them to meet me. I can't blame her for that either.*

"Brice, how long have you and my daughter known each other?"

He wanted to laugh. *Mary is the tough one? I think you guys like to divide and conquer.* He had mastered the Q&A game long ago with his own father. He wasn't worried about Lena's. "For some time now."

"Funny, I don't remember her talking about you before."

"I'm sure it slipped her mind," Brice replied. He wanted the focus off him so he turned to Gary. "I believe Lena said you have your own roofing business. How has work been?"

"Almost more business than I can keep up with at this rate. It's been a hell of a winter, and with this warmer weather, I have jobs lined up right through the fall."

"So many businesses are struggling. Glad to hear it's going well for you." He was wracking his brain and couldn't remember what she ever said Tyler did.

"You like seafood, Brice?" Tyler asked.

Bingo. Owns his own fishing boat. "I do, and your sister says you have the best catch around."

"That I do, but no one can cook better than our mother."

"You're right there, Tyler," Ernest said before turning to Brice. "Why don't you and Lena spend the night? Tomorrow I'm sure I can talk my wife into frying up some of that fish for you."

Oh, you guys are good. "I appreciate the offer Mr. Razzi—"

"Please, call me Ernest."

"Okay, Ernest. We both have work tomorrow. Maybe another time."

"What exactly did you say you do?" Ernest asked.

I didn't. "I'm a chemical engineer."

"You mean like those pharmacies?" Gary inquired.

"No. I am more specialized. I work with plastics." *Couldn't make it sound much more boring than that. I don't want anyone knowing what we do or where we do it.*

"Must be doing okay with that limo out there," Tyler said.

"It holds its own." He looked around, hoping to see Lena and Nicholas, but no one was coming to save him. If they knew who he was and why he really was here, this visit would not be going so smoothly.

Gary was talking about a roof he was doing that had collapsed over the winter due to the weight of snow. He was only half listening. Out of nowhere he heard a thud and a loud cry coming from the other room. He instantly got up and headed in that direction.

Opening the door he saw Nicholas sitting on the floor crying. Lena was already on her way to pick him up but Brice beat her to him.

Scooping him in his arms, the boy wrapped his arms around his father's neck. Brice rubbed his back and softly said, "It's okay Nicholas, Daddy's here."

The entire room went silent, including his son. He hadn't meant to say it and had no idea what possessed him to do so. He looked at Lena who now stood with her mouth wide open. Mary was looking at him, then Lena, then back to him. Ernest, on the other hand, was the only one able to speak.

"As I said before, why don't you and Lena spend the night tonight? I *think* we have a lot to discuss and a good night's rest right now is probably what we all need." He reached his hand out to Mary's. "Come along, dear, let's leave these two alone with their son." He turned to Lena and said, "You know where the guest room is."

Gary and Tyler both stood looking him over in the *don't fuck with my sister or nephew* way. He would like to reassure them he wasn't going to hurt either of them, but that was yet to be seen.

"Boys, give your sister some space. Go home."

They both went over and kissed Lena on the top of the head before heading out.

Once the three of them were alone he said, "I'm sorry. That probably wasn't the way it should have been handled."

"There really isn't a good way to say it. Showing your natural instinct of caring for our son probably was the best way possible."

"I've no idea what made me do that. I can't even remember holding a child, never mind one who was crying."

Lena laughed. "Welcome to being a father."

Brice looked at the now sleeping child in his arms. Was she right? Was it some paternal instinct that kicked in? If so, why didn't his father have it? Many times he had fallen and was injured and no one came.

"We don't have to stay if you don't want to. I understand if you feel uncomfortable."

He didn't want to be here overnight. It didn't have to do with comfort level as much as with wanting to get his son home and settled in where he belonged. *God . . . home. I can't let them go back to the hell house of an apartment they were living in. It's not safe.* There was only one place for them now and that was with him in Cambridge.

"Tell your parents thank you for the offer, but tonight, I think we need to be home."

Lena nodded and left him in the kitchen with Nicholas. For once in his life he didn't have a solid plan. He needed to make a rational decision and not be swayed by emotions. He hadn't made any promises yet, not to them or to himself. Here in this house it was going to be nearly impossible to do so.

For now, he would take them home with him. Thank goodness he had a spare bedroom for them to sleep in. Did Nicholas need a crib? He didn't have the first clue. Tomorrow he and Lena would talk about a more permanent situation. *Don't worry, Nicholas, your mother and I will figure something out.*

Chapter Twenty-One

THE RIDE BACK to Cambridge was peaceful. Nicholas slept and so did Lena. Brice on the other hand had no such luxury. His home was far from ready for a child. He wasn't worried about things being broken, that was bound to happen, but he didn't want Nicholas to get hurt. His mind was racing with a list of things he normally would have assigned to his assistant to handle. Nancy wouldn't be back for a few days, and he couldn't ask Lena to do it. He wasn't even sure what he needed. *What does a two-and-a-half-year-old like? Books? Blocks?* Probably an iPad by now. Times were changing so fast and he had no clue what to do.

A boy was a boy, surely they were all pretty much the same. While they slept he searched the Internet for as much information as he could get. Hopefully this would give him a good starting point as to what to expect. After twenty minutes he had his answer. *They're all different. Everyone has different advice. Doesn't anyone know what the hell to do?*

He put his phone back in his pocket and decided he

was going to have to learn the old-fashioned way: trial and error.

He had his mother's olive skin and dark hair. *But you look like me, kiddo.* Thank God her parents had a car seat they could use. He had learned that much from Google. Nicholas stirred in his sleep and turned toward him. Brice reached over and touched his fingers. They seemed so small and fragile. He had no idea what he had been like as a baby, but Nicholas was definitely the cutest toddler around. He laughed silently to himself. *Bragging already, Brice, and you've only known about him for a few hours.*

"What are you thinking?"

He hadn't noticed that Lena was awake. She must have been watching him as he had studied Nicholas. "Planning."

"Can you be more specific?"

Sharing with her meant opening up. He wasn't ready to do that with her again. *Not sure I ever will be.* There was a level of discussion that would need to take place because they shared a child. "You can't go back to your apartment."

"Why? I thought you said the threat was over."

Because I said so. "I don't want my son living in a place like that."

He could tell by her expression that he'd hurt her. She had been providing for Nicholas the best she could without his help. He was sure, if given another option, she wouldn't have chosen that place either. It must have been very difficult for her financially.

"It's all I can afford right now. It won't be forever. You said you would give me a letter of recommendation. That will help me find full-time employment with a good salary quickly."

"What do you mean employment? Who is going to be taking care of my son while you are running around working all hours of the day and night?" His voice was louder than he meant, and Nicholas began to wake.

"Shh. You need to be calm and quiet. You can't be so angry and loud or he will pick up on that, and it will upset him."

Lena was right. Even though Nicholas didn't understand, he would still sense the tone of the conversation. He had grown up in such an unhappy home, his father yelling all the time, he refused to do this to his son. "I'm sorry. Guess I have a lot to learn."

Lena reached over and touched his hand. "We both do."

You seem to have it all together. "What I was asking before is how do you believe you will be able to work and be there for Nicholas?"

"Brice, women work and raise children every day. What do you think I've been doing all this time?"

He wasn't sure. Her family wasn't close by.

"I take him to daycare before work and pick him up at six each night. That's why I couldn't stay late and have dinner with you."

There were a few times he had tried to get her to

stay, and she'd always replied she had plans. Now he knew what they were. "If you had told me before then—"

"Then what? You wouldn't have asked me to dinner? Slept with me? Taken me to your house by force?"

No. I still would have done all those things. I'm an asshole by nature. "Honestly, Lena, I don't know what I would have done. Probably the same thing I am doing right now."

"Which is what exactly?"

"Taking you and Nicholas to stay with me."

"I can't. I—"

"This is not up for discussion. My son is staying with me. You are welcome to stay as well. If you don't want to, that is your choice, Lena, but my son isn't going back to that apartment or any place like it. Do you understand?"

Lena gave him a brief nod then turned away. She wasn't happy, and he knew it. But right now, it wasn't about them. It was all about Nicholas.

THERE WAS NO arguing with him on the way back to his house. He held all the cards now. She still worked for him and needed that letter of recommendation or this was all for nothing. *Well, not really nothing. I've been paid well.*

So for right now, she had no choice but to stay at his home. That didn't mean she'd stay in his room. It was a huge house. They should be able to live under one roof and not get in each other's way. Of course seeing him in the office during the day and at home every night was going to make it more difficult, but it was only for a few more days. Once Nancy was back things would go back to normal.

Normal? My whole life is messed up. Any less normal and I'm going to end up on a daytime TV talk show.

"Does he usually sleep in a crib?"

"No. We didn't have room for one at the apartment so he slept with me."

"I read that's not healthy for the child or the parents."

The last thing she needed was Brice telling her what she should do with her own child. She had managed on her own for over two years and didn't need advice now. If she did, she would ask for it. "He has had enough disruption in his life this past week; he doesn't need any more changes. Your home will be a strange place to him, so he will sleep with me in the guest room."

He wasn't the only one who could be demanding and stubborn. *I can be too, for special occasions, and this is one of them.*

"For tonight, but tomorrow we will discuss other arrangements."

Brice took Nicholas from her arms and carried him upstairs to her room. He laid him gently on the bed. Lena watched as he took off one shoe then the other. Before he left, Brice gave him a kiss on the forehead.

When he turned to leave he looked at her and said, "Sleep well."

No hug. No kiss. Well, I know how he feels about me now. Lena walked over and closed the bedroom door. Earlier that night they had been snuggled up on a couch planning a night of romance. Now they . . . now she wasn't sure what they were to each other. *He is back to being cold and aloof. I doubt I'll ever have his affection again, which hurts. I'm not sure I'll survive his dismissal again. But I won't break yet. I can't. For Nicholas, I'll be stronger than ever before. For him.*

Lena went to the bed and pulled up the blanket, tucking Nicholas in. He had rolled over, and she could see he was dreaming happy thoughts as his lips curled into a smile. She was happy he didn't seem to be experiencing the stress of the day. He was too little to understand. *Damn, I don't even understand it.*

What she had feared was now over. Brice knew everything. What that meant for them as a couple wasn't important any longer. Somehow they had been able to overcome the past, but moving forward into the unknown future scared her. The only thing she was positive of was that Nicholas was the best part of them both, and she and Brice would somehow work together to ensure his happiness. She lay down next to him and closed her eyes. *Good night, Nicholas. Mommy and Daddy love . . . I love you and I know Daddy wants you.* Part of her heart was breaking; her son was never going to have the relationship her brothers had experienced with their father. Was his wanting Nicholas enough? Would he ever be able to love him? *Does he even have that in him?* She didn't know, and she wasn't sure he did either.

Chapter Twenty-Two

LENA HAD SET her alarm on her cell phone as usual but she had been up for hours before it went off. Brice's words replayed in her head throughout the night. He didn't seem to regret knowing about his son, but he hadn't liked how she'd delivered the news. *Neither had I.* That had been all within her control whether she wanted to admit it or not. By delaying it, she'd increased the hurt he must have felt by not knowing three years ago.

You've missed so much, and I'm sorry for doing that to you and Nicholas. She thought back on his first step, his first word, and even his first haircut. They were all treasured memories for her, yet Brice had none. *I have robbed you of something so precious. How can I make up for that?*

There had to be some way for her to give him some piece of the time he'd missed. She had a few videos on her phone she could show him and a scrapbook of Nicholas's first year.

A smile crossed her lips as the plan developed. She knew what she could do to make up for lost time. It would mean stopping back at her apartment, but as long as she didn't take Nicholas with her, he shouldn't have any objection. Brice was correct, it wasn't a great location. *Actually far from it, but all I can afford right now.*

She showered and dressed before waking Nicholas and getting him ready for the day. *Back to our routine. No more sleeping in for you, young man.*

Timing was different, as they weren't hopping on a bus then the subway to get him to daycare. It felt odd running around in Brice's limo, but she had no other mode of transportation at this point. And that made the morning routine so much easier. *Let's not get used to this. Soon we will be back on our own.*

It felt refreshing to be back in the office. She wasn't exactly sure why. Maybe without the secret hanging over her, she was free from worry. *Well, some at least.*

Brice knowing about Nicholas resolved one major issue. The other was what was going to happen in the next few days. Was he still going to give her the letter of recommendation that he had promised? Her future required it. *If I want to continue supporting Nicholas how I have been at least.*

For someone like Brice, money was no object and never had been. He'd been born into one of the richest families in New England. He didn't know what it felt like to worry whether you were able to pay the heating bill or the electric bill that month, and some months neither happened. For her, it was all she could think about every time she went to the grocery store or if

Nicholas needed something. At that age, it seemed like he wore an outfit once then out grew it. She was positive Brice had never entered, never mind shopped at, a secondhand store. *We couldn't have made it this far without one.* A secure position wouldn't fix everything but it would be a life-changer for them financially at least. With coffee in hand she headed to Brice's door and knocked even though it was open.

"Come in."

Feeling confident, she entered his office and approached his desk. When she went to hand him the coffee, he snapped.

"What the hell are you doing here? You should be home," he yelled as though she were in another room instead of only feet away.

"Excuse me? I work here, remember?" She wasn't going to let him bully her. Not here or anywhere. He might be rich and powerful, but she should still be treated with respect. *Don't push too hard. You don't have the letter yet.*

Brice came around the desk and took the coffee from her. "Not anymore."

Surprised by his words, she asked, "Why? Was there something I did wrong? Did Nancy return?"

"Where is Nicholas?"

"At daycare."

Brice shook his head. "My son is not being raised by a bunch of strangers."

She wanted to ease his mind, tell him that this was

only for the short-term, but that wouldn't be the truth. She worked and was going to for many years, which meant daycare while he's young and then after-school programs as he grew up. "Brice, he is fine. He's with a great staff, and he is happily playing with other children his age."

"Do I need to repeat it again? My son is not being raised by strangers."

It was such a common occurrence that he shouldn't have been surprised or opposed to it. Something didn't feel right. Was there more to it than Nicholas? If so, what?

There's only one way to find out. "Brice, we are two grown adults who should be able to sit and discuss things in a mature manner. No yelling, demanding, or threatening each other."

He didn't respond, only stood there waiting for her answer. *Damn you're stubborn. But so am I.*

"So what do you know about daycare?" *Probably nothing.*

Brice arched a brow. "I don't need to know anything about daycare to make a decision about my son."

"Funny. You always make your decisions based on facts and research. Yet when it comes to Nicholas you've decided to guess what is best opposed to *knowing* what is?" *That should do it.* Lena felt proud of herself for pulling that one out. How could he dispute logic? He lived by it.

"Well played, Lena. You're correct. I don't know anything about that. That doesn't mean I don't know what I want for my son. So let me ask you a few questions."

Oh shit. Here it comes. She should have guessed he wouldn't bend to her without a fight, and the odds of her winning one were slim to none. "Ask away."

"Who was there for you when you fell and got hurt? Who put you down for your nap? Who read you a bedtime story? Who—?"

"I get the point. My mother." Lena's voice became soft. "She was always there whenever I needed her." *And still is.*

Brice stood with his arms crossed over his chest and a smug look as though claiming victory. This was far from over. She wasn't her mother, and she didn't have a man providing for her so she could be home with her child either. Saying it that way was only going to stir the pot. No, she needed to think of something he would under-stand. *Money? No. Success? Maybe. Come on Lena, think.*

"My mother taught me something very valuable. Although she was home with us, she had yearned to be out growing as a person. She didn't regret being with us, but she missed out on so much, and so did we. My brother Gary was so shy with strangers that he used to cry if my mother needed to leave him for five minutes. There is good and bad in both options. As long as the time you have with your children is quality time, it doesn't have to be twenty-four/seven."

"I'm glad you see it that way. There are, however, children who are left to be cared for by many different people and never get the feeling of family, or belonging."

There was something in his eyes when he spoke that said they were no longer speaking of Nicholas. She knew he had a difficult relationship with his father, but he'd never spoken of a mother, a home life. Like he had said before, sharing was not his strength. *But it can be learned. Maybe I could teach him.*

"Whether raised by someone else or a parent, sometimes the scars are visible, sometimes not. The ones hidden are usually the worst because we not only hide them from others, but we hide them from ourselves. Healing and growth only happens when you acknowledge the scars." *When did I start talking so deeply and philosophically?*

Brice laughed. "You really think you're going to win? I have no problem listening to your beautiful voice all day, but don't try getting all philosophical on me. It won't work. Why don't you face the fact that I believe he needs his mother home with him."

Lena didn't want to say it, but the truth was all she had left. "Your reality and mine are different, Brice. I don't have the luxury of staying home. I have bills to pay, food to buy, and rent to worry about. None of these are going to magically disappear."

"Is that what you're worried about? Money? I have every intention of supporting my son. Money is not an issue."

It felt like a slap in her face. *How dare he?* He thought he could open his wallet and buy her son? Prior to having Nicholas, she had lived in a better apartment, but had been frugal. Her small savings from working fulltime in the years after college had been stretched to pay the hospital bills when she had Nicholas, and to set them up in their current apartment. She had been working hard for the last three years and had been wise with her money. Childcare wasn't cheap, but she was keeping her head above water. Just. *How dare he waltz into our lives and minimalize all I have achieved on my own?* With Brice in the picture, was all her hard work for nothing? *No way.* "Brice, it might not be what you think is best for Nicholas but I have been doing a great job of providing for him so far. Granted it might not meet your almighty standards, but he is loved, healthy, and happy. Which one of those do you think your money can buy?"

Lena didn't wait for his answer. Whatever putdown he was about to make about her provisions thus far could be said to the dead air. *He's only wanted me for sex. Other than that I mean nothing to him. That is all too clear now. I have always been beneath him in his eyes and always will be.* She had work to do to finish off her week. *Whether he gives me that damn recommendation or not.*

YOU ARE ONE spunky one. He was not used to anyone speaking to him in such a way. If it was anyone else he would have thrown them out on their ass. But Lena only said what was from her heart. Not that it made it any better.

He had been tempted to follow her and let her know

that last little speech didn't change a thing, but it had. She was right. Who was he to come into their lives now and tell them what needed to change? He didn't want strangers raising Nicholas. He had more nannies than he could remember. Those women brought him up, not his father. If she was warm and friendly to them, she was gone. If she coddled them in any way, she was gone. Any acts of kindness or love and—*I'm not my father.*

Brice grabbed his coffee and left the office. Lena was sitting at her desk. By the look on her face she was ready for something rude or demeaning to come out of his mouth. *She knows me well.*

"I'll be in the lab for a few hours if anyone is looking for me. We can pick up Nicholas together on our way home tonight. There are a few necessities I thought we could stop and check out."

Lena blinked in surprise and only nodded.

Ah, I think I finally got in the last word. He held back his laugh. He knew if he didn't somehow she would make him pay for it later.

The compound was ready to go. All he needed was Asher's final decision on location. Right now he should be returning calls to the list of names and numbers Lena had given him, some he already knew he had no interest in speaking with. There was only one he wanted to speak to. *Sophie Barrington.* It had been a long time since they'd spoken. *Too long.* For years it had seemed as if he lived there, not with his father. *How I wish we were there, all six of us.*

Dialing the number that hadn't changed over all these years, he waited to hear a familiar voice.

"Barrington residence, this is Emily."

Who the hell is Emily? That name didn't sound like anyone in the family that he remembered. "Is Sophie available?"

"Sorry, she is on her cell phone right now, would you like to leave a message?"

Sounds more like calling an office than a home. "Sure. Tell her Brice Henderson will be attending the art auction and will be bringing a guest, Lena Razzi."

"Wonderful. Thank you so much for your support. I look forward to meeting you and Ms. Razzi at that time. I will pass along your message."

The woman hung up so quickly he didn't get a chance to ask who she was. *Emily. Why does that name sound familiar?* Then he recalled Lena informing him it was Emily Harris who was building the museum for the blind. *Talk about a woman who thinks outside the box. Way outside.*

Looking through the list, he didn't see anyone else he wanted to speak to. *Not at the moment at least.* Opening his computer he did something he had never done before and never thought he would do: search for a boy's bedroom set.

He debated going with the standard dark cherry boring set like he had but then his eye caught a bed that had a frame built like a race car. The hood of the car opened and turned into a slide, and the tires opened to reveal shelves to store toys. *Where was this stuff when I was growing up?* Brice didn't stop there. His search revealed every crazy type of bed one could imagine. From castles to dragons. Every once in a while he would click on one and find it was for a girl, for a princess. *Next one needs to be a girl.*

What the fuck? He would have punched anyone who would have said he was having one child, never mind letting a second one cross his mind. *The next one?* The thought shocked him. He hadn't planned on one, had no idea what being a full-time parent meant. He knew he wanted what the Barringtons had, but that didn't mean he could do it. They were different people. Two parents with one goal. He and Lena couldn't seem to agree on anything. *Except in the bedroom.* But that wasn't going to make a good home for one child, let alone more.

He closed the laptop and left the lab. He was spending too much time dealing with the material things, not what was important. *Time.*

When he went to the office again Lena was on the phone. "Yes, Mr. West. I'll be sure to give him your message. Yes, I understand. I'm sure he will call you at his earliest convenience. Have a good day."

She handled those calls almost as well as Nancy. If she only could learn how to be mean and tell them off she would be perfect. *But you're already perfect in my eyes. Don't change.* She was what every man would want by his side. The problem wasn't her. It was him. He was the last thing she needed.

"Brice. Did you need something?"

"Yes. Let's get out of here. Tell the answering service to take calls until the end of the week."

"I thought we discussed this. I'm not quitting."

"Good. Now as a good employee, do as I say."

Lena picked up the phone and dialed the number. He listened as she gave them the information as he directed.

"Now what?" Lena asked.

He reached out and took her hand. "It's too beautiful to sit inside. Let's go pick up our son. Have you taken him to the children's museum yet?"

Lena shook her head. "Are you feeling okay, Brice?"

He wasn't sure. He knew he didn't feel like himself. If this was a good or bad thing was unclear. He hadn't changed. Business and success meant everything to him, but what would a few days off change? On Monday, Nancy would be back in the office, and everything would be back to normal. *It's only a few days. Nothing more.*

Chapter Twenty-Three

L ENA HAD NO idea what had gotten into Brice. One minute he'd been telling her to be a stay-at-home mother, the next he was taking time off to spend with Nicholas. She had no doubt this was going to be short-lived. There was an unforeseen lull in his work at this time but once Asher gave the go-ahead, it would be back to normal. *Living and breathing the job and nothing else will matter.*

It was good she realized that. That way Lena didn't set herself up for heartache later when he no longer showed any interest. There had been a few changes at his home, but none that affected her.

Nicholas now had his own bedroom, one that looked more like an apartment. It had everything a child could imagine and more. He spent hours going up and down the slide until he finally laid himself down on his bed and decided it was time for a nap.

He had always slept with her, mostly due to lack of space in their apartment. He was in the room next to hers, and she had the baby monitor on all night, but she felt lost without him. It hadn't hit her until that first night alone that she needed him as much as he needed her.

Each night when they put Nicholas to bed, Lena thought for sure Brice would try making a move on her. She missed the nearness of him, and she was sure he must feel the same. There were things that weren't important now, and an active sex life was definitely at the bottom of the list. *With me.* It was one more thing that, once he was bored with it, he brushed to the side. *And I'm one of those things. Is that what happened three years ago? He'd simply become bored with me?*

The remainder of the week was like a family vacation. Brice never went to the office. Of course neither did she. Every day they went on a new adventure. Some big, some small, but always together. They didn't talk about the future, about family, or anything permanent. She wanted to bring it up. She wanted to talk about what comes next, but each time she hinted at the subject he cut her off.

She had been awake most of the night, and morning had already come. What she knew would happen, did. Brice got up long before dawn and slipped off to work. The happy little family unit they'd had was over. Reality was back. Today it was just Nicholas and her. *We were okay before, and we will be again. Is it time to move back to my apartment? Is that what Brice wants?*

BEING BACK AT work felt good. A few days without a

routine was nice yet unnerving. Every time he was near Lena he felt himself slipping, wanting her more and more. The best and worst times were watching her with Nicholas. He had always known she was a special person. Loving, caring, and gentle. *Everything I'm not.* But when he watched her with Nicholas, she blossomed into the most amazing woman. She was a natural teacher and had the patience of a saint.

Nicholas had had an occasional tantrum on the floor because he was overtired when Brice had kept him up past his nap. Lena knew exactly how to calm him without giving in to his bad behavior. Within minutes, Nicholas was fast asleep and all was well again. Growing up, if he was crying his father would have said, "Wipe those tears or I'll really give you something to cry about." The reason behind tears didn't matter. Injury, sickness, or loneliness, the end result had always been the same. *And there had been many times he had given us something to cry about.*

Brice had feared an abusive father was something passed down genetically. Scientifically, that shouldn't be possible, but that was why he'd chosen to never have children. *A reason why I ended it with Lena all those years ago. I knew she wanted a family. She deserved a family.* He slammed his fist on his desk. *They both deserve someone better than what I can give them.*

He didn't need to work late, but he did anyway. It was time for them to get back to the way things were, the way they had always been and always would be. It wasn't going to be easy, not for him or either of them, but it would be the best for Lena and Nicholas in the long run. People like him were meant to be alone. *For their sake, not mine.*

"What are you doing here so late, Brice? I thought you would be going home by now."

"Nancy, when have you ever seen me leave before nine?"

Nancy shook her head. "I was hoping . . ."

Brice arched his brow. "Hoping what? That your little matchmaking game would work?"

"You know about that?" Nancy admitted.

"You're lucky you are invaluable to me or your ass would be on unemployment and I would make sure no one would hire you again."

Nancy laughed. "Oh, if I had a dollar for every time you said that to me."

"Glad you find this humorous. I don't. My personal life is just that. Personal."

"Yes, Mr. Henderson. Whatever you say, Mr. Henderson," Nancy said in a joking tone as she turned and headed back to her desk. "If you don't mind, I am leaving, as I *do* have a life outside of B&H and I'd like to keep it that way."

Good to have you back, Nancy. You're such a pain in the ass. I've missed you. With the office now silent he was left with nothing but his own thoughts and they led him to the one place he didn't want to go. *Lena.*

It had been more than a week since he'd tasted her,

held her in his arms. His cock was aching to be in her. Did she purposely wear tight jeans that hugged her perfectly round ass? And why did she always bend over in front of him? Was she trying to kill him? Didn't she realize his control was starting to break? If he didn't stay away today he knew he would have her tonight.

That's not happening since it's my turn at the hospital. He needed an update from the one person who seemed to give a damn.

"Zoey. Any change?"

"Brice, good news. He is awake, not saying much, but awake. Are you still coming tonight? It's been a long day, and I need a break."

"I'll be there shortly."

Before putting his phone away he texted Lena. "Not coming home tonight. Say good night to Nicholas for me."

Being an asshole comes so naturally to me. Will she wonder where I am? Will she assume I'm at the hospital, or with someone else?

The night at the hospital was anything but usual. Zoey said their father wasn't talking much. The entire time Brice was there he talked nonstop. Nothing Brice wanted to hear. Things he could never repeat. Things about him and his siblings. *We're even more fucked up than anyone can imagine.*

Was it his father's way of messing with him one last time? He shared with Brice why he'd acted the way he had. What his childhood had been like. *And I thought you were bad, Dad. You had it worse than we did.* That didn't make anything better. Understanding where he came from actually seemed to make it worse. There was no way he could share this with his brothers and Zoey. It was best that it died with him. *And now I carry the burden of this knowledge. This sick fucking knowledge. Is this a sign that I have no right to be a father? How can I be a fit father knowing where I come from?*

No matter how hard it was to process all the shit just unloaded onto him, it didn't change the fact that his father had lost the battle. His heart gave out. His suffering was over. *And mine begins.*

He called his sister and gave her the news. "Dad's gone." What he didn't understand was why she broke down crying. Dad had been so mean, so abusive to her. *God, I'm not even sure he knew she existed.* But with what his dad had just shared, he understood why. She represented everything he'd hated. *We all do, but most of all Zoey.*

Brice needed a drink. Leaving the hospital, he went to the one place he knew he could escape reality. *Home . . . to Lena.*

Chapter Twenty-Four

NICHOLAS WAS FAST asleep in his room, and with Brice not coming home there was no reason she shouldn't take advantage of the huge tub in his master bedroom. *One bubble bath won't hurt anything, and he won't ever have to know.*

It wasn't like there was a horrible bathroom in his home, but the guest room only had a shower. It was very nice, better than anything she would ever have, but she'd always liked a tub. *Soft music, lots of bubbles, and a glass of wine.* Sliding in so only her head was out of the water, she moaned. *Heaven.*

It had been a long day. After only a few days of Brice being around, Nicholas had adapted quickly. His new routine of "follow Daddy and copy everything he is doing" didn't happen today. He was whiny and looked lost. Lena knew he was missing his daddy. Brice probably didn't comprehend the impact he was having on Nicholas. *It's his loss. Enjoy your job, Brice. I'm glad you have something that makes you happy, but don't hurt my boy.*

This was all new territory. She wasn't sure what to

do. Normally she would call brother Gary and talk things through. For a guy he really was a good listener. But this wasn't something he could relate to. He was single, no children. What could a bachelor tell her that could help? *I really need to speak to Mom. I don't need her to solve my problems, but I would value her counsel. Maybe tomorrow.* She knew she owed her parents an explanation as to why she had hidden Brice's paternity for so long. She was sure her parents thought she didn't know the father's name since she had refused to tell them. That was never the issue. If they had known, they would have forced the issue and maybe Brice would have turned his back on them a second time. Lena believed things worked out the way they were supposed to if you didn't try forcing them. Brice may have lost two years with Nicholas, but she had to believe they would make up for it now.

The soft music was food for her soul, and the hot water eased her aching muscles. She didn't know there were tubs that kept the temperature the same from start to end. *Like I needed another reason not to get out.*

She closed her eyes and let the music flow through her. It was a song she remembered dancing to with Brice one night long ago. They had traveled to Newport to hear some band jam. A local band had been competing. Brice hadn't wanted to go, but back then he did a lot of things he didn't want to. Mostly because it made her happy. Now he does only what he wants. She wasn't sure that made him happy. There were a few times when she thought the spark of life that was once there had returned. But as quickly as it appeared, it disappeared. No, Brice was anything but happy.

Was there something she could do to help him find his way? *Did he want to find happiness?* Lena had read that some people liked to be miserable. She didn't know anyone like that. Mostly because if they were negative people she cut them out of her life. It was hard enough to stay positive without surrounding yourself with people waiting to bring you down all the time.

So why do I still want to be with Brice? He was the only person who had ever hurt her that deeply. Left her crushed emotionally. He also was the only person who had made her feel so alive. When they were together he had treated her as a special jewel. Something had happened to change it so abruptly. Even now she didn't fully understand what caused their breakup. If she erased that nightmare from her mind for good, she would be left remembering a wonderful love story.

And there she had her answer. Through the pain, one thing survived. *My love for him.* No matter what transpired between them—the arguments, the misunderstandings, having a child—nothing made her stop loving him. The only reason he was able to hurt her so badly was because she loved him so much. *Life's cruel joke. Well, I'm going to get the last laugh; I'm still standing. You haven't won.*

But how far will I allow him to hurt me? If he never loves me back, but finds someone else to warm his bed, how will I cope with that? She could see living with him was not something she should continue to do. He didn't want her. He might enjoy her sexually, but that wasn't enough for her. She wanted the fairy tale, her beloved, her other half. That wasn't in Brice's plan and goals he had set for himself. There was no room for her, at least not the way she wanted. She needed to face the facts. This wasn't going to be a permanent thing. Soon, they would go their separate ways, but at least Nicholas would have two parents now who loved him. *Something good came out of all this.*

Taking another sip of wine, she reached to put it back on the edge of the tub. It slipped and fell to the bathmat. *Oh shit. How am I going to explain red wine on his white rug?*

Getting out of the tub she bent over and tried to wipe off as much as she could.

It was getting worse. The rug was stained with the red wine and the floor was getting wetter as bubbles slid down her body to the floor.

"So much for sneaking in a quick bath."

"And here I thought you were waiting for me," Brice's husky voice said from the doorway.

Naked, she turned to meet his gaze. The hunger in his eyes burned her flesh. Every part of her brain told her to turn away. They shouldn't do this, not again. It would only complicate things more. But she couldn't move.

"I thought you weren't coming home."

"I'm glad I did." His eyes traveled her full length,

and her body reacted.

"I should go to my room." Her voice shook with desire.

Brice stepped closer and gently touched her chin, tipping her face to look at him. "You should stay with me." Pulling her against him, she could feel his arousal, and that left little question as to what he wanted.

As he bent to kiss her, she felt her legs tremble. *Please. Don't. We shouldn't.* She wanted to stop him but the words were lost as his lips claimed hers. Slowly at first, as though he had never kissed her before. He traced her lips with his tongue, teasing and encouraging them to open for him, which they did. He was driving her over the edge with only his kisses. If she didn't stop now, she wouldn't be able to. Need roared through her body. She wanted him like she had never wanted him before.

His hands cupped her breasts and pinched her nipples softly. Lena moaned into his mouth as he kissed her. *God, I need you, Brice.*

His mouth left hers and trailed kisses slowly down her neck, to her collarbone, and finally stopped at her breast. Taking one nipple gently in his mouth, he sucked and nibbled. When she thought she couldn't take any more, he moved his attention to her other breast, repeating the process.

"Lena, I want to taste every inch of you."

The heat in the pit of her stomach flowed through the rest of her body. He picked her up in his arms and carried her to his bed. He undressed and joined her.

Both stood naked and hot with need.

There was no stopping now, and she didn't want it to. She wanted him, loved him, and needed him. Reaching out, she pushed him back onto the bed.

"First I taste you." She slowly ran her fingers up the front of his legs, over his hips, and finally on his swollen shaft that was begging for her lips. Never turning her eyes from his, her tongue darted out and licked the tip, then blew gently on it. A husky groan rumbled through him.

"Oh God, Lena."

His body tensed as her tongue continued to lick the length of him and back to the tip. His soft gray eyes darkened as he watched her. She loved knowing the effect she was having on him. It increased her own desire. He let out a deep growl as she took him deep within her mouth, stroking him with one hand and sucking him, teasing the head with her tongue before going deep again. Her need grew, so did her rhythm, faster and more aggressive. No longer giving, she was now taking what she wanted. His hands tangled in her long dark curly hair as he guided her head faster, deeper. His moans grew louder, proof she was driving him crazy. The more he moaned the more she was turned on. She knew it wouldn't be long before she claimed her prize.

Then in one quick movement he pulled away, his breathing ragged. "If you don't stop, I won't be able to hold back."

Brice grabbed her by her wrist and pulled her onto

him then rolled over so she lay beneath him. "Now I taste you." His kisses were fierce as he made his way lower, over her flat stomach then the tops of her thighs. Parting her legs with one hand he had full access to her delicate folds.

His fingers parted her so his tongue could lick her clit. Her body shuddered as his tongue darted in and out again and again. Then he circled her clit, sending her mind whirling. "You taste so sweet." His words echoed through her. She fisted the sheets beneath her when he sucked her harder. Cries of pleasure filled the room. *Oh God, this feels so good.* When she thought it couldn't feel any better he inserted a finger inside her, sending her body in waves of a climax that rocked her. She clenched around him as her release continued. "Yes. Oh yes."

Her body still pulsing from the first wave, she felt his breath warm against her neck when he whispered, "You don't know how badly I want to feel you wrapped around me." He pulled away slightly, but she held him in place with her legs.

She felt him thick and hot, teasing her entrance. "Please, Brice. I need you now," she begged.

"I don't want to hurt you, but I need you so badly." His voice filled with need.

Lifting her hips to him she offered herself. He entered her in a swift thrust. He was large, but she was wet and ready for him. Her body welcomed him. *Yes!* She rocked her hips against him, meeting each thrust with her own.

He rode her hard and fast. Both of them hungry for more and each willing to give it. He cupped her breasts holding them so he could suck her nipples, never losing a beat. He nipped her nipple and her body went wild. "Please, Brice. I need to—" Her climax came stronger than the one before.

"Yes. Oh fuck, yes." His voice was husky as his body joined hers.

She tried biting her lip to contain her screams, but he seized them with his own as she felt him shudder against her one final time before they collapsed into each other's arms.

They both lay there gasping for breath with their legs tangled together. She tried to move but Brice held her to him. He kissed her forehead and said, "Stay with me tonight."

She was about to tell him she couldn't but there was something in his voice that sounded desperate. "Brice—"

"Please, Lena. Don't ask. Just stay with me tonight. That's all I'm asking. One night."

She would stay, because he needed her and because she couldn't bring herself to leave. *One night is all you're asking for, but I need so much more.*

ALTHOUGH HE WAS exhausted and his eyes were closed, sleep didn't come. His father's words haunted him. If his intentions were to share all his dirty little secrets so he could die with a clear conscious, then he should have asked for a minister, not one of his children. *And defi-*

nitely not me.

For many years they all had been asking questions: *Why do you hate us so much? What happened to make you so mean? What happened to our mother?* The answers had now been provided, but never had he thought the truth would be so fucking ugly.

Brice had always tried to protect the others from their father's wrath whether it was verbal or physical. With his death, he should no longer need to do so, but now he knew differently. He never wanted them to feel what he was feeling right now. An emotional war was taking place within him. Part of him was glad his father was gone; the abusive legacy had ended. Now he only felt sorrow for everything he'd learned about his father's past.

Last week he'd been bitching to Lena that a mother's place was home with her children. After hearing what severe abuse his father had suffered at the hands of their grandmother, he wished his father had been raised by nannies or placed in daycare. No one could have damaged a person's psyche any more than his grandmother had. *I had always wanted more family. But I'm glad we never knew her.*

Brice wasn't sure if she was alive or dead, however, it didn't matter. If she was half as bad as what his father told him, he wanted nothing to do with her.

Finding his mother on the other hand was going to be challenging and maybe impossible, but he would try. Once he found her, he could decide if he would share the information with his siblings. Until he was convinced she would bring something good into their lives—that they would actually benefit from knowing her—she would remain a mystery to them. *We've all suffered enough in this family. It had to end eventually. Let it end here with me.*

He pulled Lena's naked body closer to his. He couldn't be alone tonight and needed comforting. No one else could have substituted for Lena at this moment. *Perhaps never.*

His hope that the two of them could continue with a casual love affair without any future commitment ended abruptly for him once he found out they had a child. It didn't matter how much he cared about her or wanted her. He thought he knew what kind of fucked-up family he came from and never wanted to pass that along to another generation. *That's probably why none of us are married or have children. We all have the same fear. I just have to make sure my fear doesn't become a reality.*

The only way to ensure that was to keep a safe distance from them. *The closer we are, the more I can hurt her, and I refuse to do that. Not again. Never again.*

But he broke his own rule and took her to his bed. He wanted to blame her, say it was her fault for being so fucking hot, sexy, *and* naked in his bathroom, but he knew he had come home and sought her out. He had already stopped by her room and Nicholas's before coming to his own. The sight of her standing naked in his bathroom brought him to a point of no return. His rational thinking of what was best for them was blinded by his pure physical need for her.

But was it only that? If so, then why didn't he let her leave when they were done? *God, I practically begged her to stay with me. What's wrong with me? Why can't I let her go?*

He had done it before. Cut all ties with her, and for her sake, had hoped they never saw each other again. Now it was impossible to do so, as their bond was forever through Nicholas. All he could do was protect them from what may lie within him.

When morning came, it would be the start of a new beginning. They would need to go back to how it had been before last night, cohabitate without having a physical relationship. It wouldn't be easy for him, and probably wouldn't be for Lena either, but it meant they could raise their son together. *Should I even be doing this?* He knew they both deserved more—better—but that was all he could give. *I'm giving you my best, but I am far from worthy of having you both in my life. It would be wiser if you left.*

Chapter Twenty-Five

THE NEXT FEW days were filled with meeting with attorneys to decide what would happen to Poly-Shyn. His father's will had left it equally to all six children. The problem was no one wanted it. Zoey had stepped in to manage it when he had entered the hospital, but going forward was beyond her capabilities.

It was their family legacy, and each one of them agreed it wasn't something they wanted to continue. That meant finding the right buyer. There were a lot of people who seemed to be hovering, waiting to devour it. This was not their expertise at all. Thankfully he had an old friend who made his fortune acquiring and selling companies like Poly-Shyn.

"Trent, thanks for taking my call. Have I heard correctly that you're married with a son now?"

"And a second one on the way," Trent replied.

"I don't know how you manage to do it all, not with the lifestyle you live."

Trent laughed. "*Lived* would be the correct term. Funny how children change you. My father told me if your life doesn't drastically change when you become a father then you're not doing it right."

Brice hadn't ever heard that saying before, but it sounded damn good. *The question is, can I change?* He never expected to see Trent married, especially with a family. He and Asher were so much alike. They took what they wanted and crushed anything they couldn't have. Not what he considered a great role model as a dad. "Your wife must be amazing to be able to put up with your ass."

"That she is. So I don't think you called to chat about family, not that I mind. What's going on?"

"The family business. We want it gone."

"You mean sold, right? I no longer deal in . . . should we say, assisting companies to close their doors."

It was Brice's turn to laugh. "Yeah, sold. You really are a crazy son of a bitch."

"You don't know the half of it. Hey, I'm going to be in your neck of the woods in a few days for some art auction my wife Elaine wants to attend. Why don't I give you a call then?"

"Is this Sophie Barrington's event?"

"That's the one. You going?"

"I will be there, and I believe my sister and a few brothers. If we have a few minutes maybe that would be a good time to talk."

"Sounds good. Don't let my wife know; she thinks this is a little getaway before the baby is born, and trust me, you don't want to see her angry when she is pregnant."

"Deal."

With everything else going on, he had let the auction slip his mind. *Did I even tell Lena we're going? Probably not. Why would I? That's the nice thing to do, and God knows I'm not nice.*

He thought about telling her that day, but remembered it wasn't only the two of them to think of. What about Nicholas? He didn't know anyone who could watch him. He hadn't even told his family yet. *Good thing we don't drop in on each other. It would be hard to miss the gym set in my backyard near the pool.*

Picking up his phone he called Lena.

"Is something wrong?"

"No, why?"

"Brice, you never call during the day. If anything, you text me to check on Nicholas."

He hadn't realized how far he had taken it. Each time he heard her voice it felt like a blow to the gut. *It's better that way. Let her hate me.* "You had mentioned the art auction. I responded that you and I will be attending. Do you think your parents would mind watching Nicholas for a night or two?"

He had been nearby a few times when they were chatting on the phone. Each time they asked when they were coming down. He was sure they would be willing to keep him even longer if given the option.

"Did you forget one thing?"

He searched but came up empty. "No. Not that I can

think of."

Sarcastically she said, "Exactly. You don't think, do you? We are not a couple, Brice. Even if we were, you cannot assume that I will attend anything with you. You should have asked me prior to responding for me."

He was the eldest child and the boss of his own company, therefore, that was how he behaved in most situations. Lena was one of the few people who wouldn't tolerate it. It was refreshing most times. This wasn't one of them. "You're right. I will work on that." *No promise I'll change.* "So can you please call and ask them if they can watch Nicholas for us?" The phone went silent. He knew she was still there as he could hear the tapping of her shoe on the marble floor. *Oh, she's pissed.*

There was dead silence. Was she considering her options? He knew she wanted to be there, even it if wasn't with him, she had indicated her interest in this event.

"I'll ask," Lena replied then hung up the phone.

Her tone said it all. She was giving in to his request, but she was far from happy about it. *My methods aren't nice, but they get results.*

"Mom, I promise, Brice and I will stay for dinner when we pick up Nicholas." *If he can answer for me, then turn around is fair play.*

"Good. Your father and I would like to get to know your young man better."

He's not my anything. When I spoke with her and apologized for rushing off that night, she had been understanding. She hadn't berated me for not telling Brice about Nicholas, but I had heard her disappointment. She didn't want to tell her mother that Brice and she were not a couple. She didn't want her mother's pity or her criticism. It was what it was, and as much as it was hurting her, she knew nothing would change. "Please, Mom, don't embarrass me. Brice doesn't like to talk about personal stuff, and let's just say, you don't always know when to draw the line."

"Well, Lena, since you refused to tell us anything about him for all these years, how else do you expect us to get to know him?"

Point taken. "Okay, but just go easy on him. He is a bit . . . well, he's . . . not used to a family like ours."

"I'll be on my best behavior. I promise."

Oh, that scares me. When her mother spoke like that it meant she had been plotting what she was going to say for some time. *Brice, you're on your own. Consider it payback.*

She had told her mother that Brice wasn't used to a family like theirs, yet she really didn't know what he was used to. While working in his office, she had spoken to a few of his brothers on the phone. They'd sounded normal and she knew a bit more about Zoey, who was such a sweet girl. *A bit pushy, and far from shy, but still sweet.* What she didn't understand was why he hadn't introduced them to her or more importantly to their son. She may be nothing to Brice, but Nicholas was family. Wouldn't he want his son to know his aunt and uncles?

God knows I do. The more the merrier.

If there was a reason he kept them hidden away, he hadn't shared it with her. Maybe he was embarrassed about them, about Nicholas. *Oh God, no.* That thought hurt. She had kept him away all these years and maybe Brice was too embarrassed to tell anyone. It wasn't his doing; it had been hers. She was sure if he had known about Nicholas he would have stepped up to the plate and taken care of him right from day one. *Financially anyway.*

Who am I kidding? I don't think he knows what he would've done, so how can I even begin to guess? She knew she needed to stop thinking of what could have been. The only thing that mattered now was the future. *And with the little information you are sharing regarding that, Brice, it's as unclear as the past.*

The only thing she did know was her feelings for him. She thought it was hard before, being away from a man she loved and raising their son on her own. *That's nothing compared to living in the same house and never being able to tell him how I feel because he'll only shut down again as he did three years ago. For Nicholas's sake, I must endure this torture. But is Nicholas actually benefitting if his father is always at work anyway?*

Chapter Twenty-Six

L ENA HATED TO admit it but this had the potential of being the perfect date night. Brice had taken her out for dinner at a quiet, almost romantic spot. She had been hopeful, but he seemed so distracted. Little to no conversation had taken place between them, as he was preoccupied with his cell phone. Although the restaurant had been lovely and the food excellent, the company had left her wanting. She could only hope whatever was troubling him would be resolved before they arrived at the auction.

Thankfully her worries were for nothing. Once they arrived, the tension within him seemed to vanish. They looked at several pieces of artwork together before someone came by and asked to speak to Brice. Since Brice wanted to rush through each piece she actually was happy to be able to view them alone and appreciate the masterpieces they were.

And the artwork blew her mind. Ever since Sophie had called and given her information regarding museums for the blind, she had spent hours researching them.

They were quickly coming around to display not only works of art that the blind could enjoy but also the artwork they had created.

As she went from one piece to another she was in awe. *I can't do this and I have perfect vision.*

Lena spent more than thirty minutes speaking to Emily Harris regarding her mother's work as well as the clay sculptures Emily had created. She was a strong woman who had a vision and was determined to see it through. Lena respected that. *I wish I knew where I was headed. Every time I think I know it, something changes.*

She looked around the room for Brice. He was with Zoey and a few other men. She was tempted to go over, but they looked like they were talking business. *Can't you ever relax and enjoy yourself, Brice? Not even for one night?*

Zoey must have seen her watching them, and she came over to join her.

"You get my brothers together in one room and everything else seems to fade away. Guess that's what happens when you only see each other once a year."

His brothers? His family is here? She felt sick to her stomach knowing they were so close, yet he hadn't introduced her. *I feel like a dirty, sordid secret.* The night, which had felt so pleasant a moment ago, changed. Lena couldn't look. It only hurt her more. She turned and pretended not to have heard Zoey's comment. *Damn you, Brice. Damn you.*

"Have you talked to Emily Harris yet?"

"Yes, I have. Nice girl."

"I hear she is seeing Asher Barrington. Can you believe that? What is a nice girl like her doing with such an arrogant jackass?" Zoey asked softly.

I'm not one to question her judgment. "I haven't met Mr. Barrington in person, but I spoke to him on the phone once." *That was more than enough for me.* He could see why Asher and Brice were business partners. Both driven by success.

"I could ask Brice this, but it won't get me anywhere, so I guess I'll ask you."

Please don't. The last thing she wanted was to be put on the spot. She had years of experience deflecting things like this with her own family. She didn't want to start using it on his. "I most likely won't have an answer for you. I suggest talking to your brother."

Zoey laughed. "Brice? Share anything with anyone? I thought you knew him better than that."

Oh I do, but you don't need to know that. "No. Not really."

Zoey looked at Lena then to Brice and back to Lena. "Well, for someone who isn't interested in my brother, he sure seems to be interested in you. He hasn't taken his eyes off you all night. Who can blame him? You look stunning in that red dress. Besides, you're happy with your partner and little boy, so perhaps he is taking this opportunity to watch you. I had really thought you'd be the one. I can't be right all the time, can I?"

Lena tried to resist but couldn't. She had turned and as Zoey said, Brice was watching her. *He probably wants to know what we are talking about. Has to know everything. That's all, nothing more.*

She heard someone call Zoey from across the room. "Sorry, got to run. Nice talking with you. Maybe we can do lunch again sometime?"

Or maybe not. The last time you grilled me. "Sounds nice."

It was refreshing to be alone for a moment. This event was supposed to be relaxing; instead she found it filled with the rich and powerful, all pretending as though they weren't speaking business, but everyone knew they were.

"Are you enjoying the event?"

Lena turned to see a tall woman elegantly dressed even in her pregnant state. "Yes, I am. And you?"

"I wouldn't have missed this for anything. Emily Harris has a vision so inspiring, and New Hampshire isn't far at all. I already informed my husband, Trent, that once it's up and running we have to go." She extended her hand. "I'm Elaine Davis. And the gentleman pretending not to be speaking business with your date is my husband, Trent."

My date. Ha! "Nice to meet you. I'm Lena Razzi."

Lena knew his name from the tabloids. He'd had one hell of a reputation before he'd married. How anyone tamed him was beyond her. *If Trent and Asher can find love maybe there is hope for Brice and me.*

She didn't want to start hoping or wishing for anything though. It would only lead to more heartbreak.

Lena had to accept where they were now. *Just because a few of these women found their happily ever after doesn't mean everyone does. Some of us don't even come close.*

Lena spent the remainder of the evening meeting more people she never thought she'd see in person. Elaine was kind enough to introduce her to her husband and then to Dominic Corisi and his wife, Abby. She might not be on Brice's arm where she had longed to be, but she was having a wonderful time, and everyone was so welcoming.

Not that she didn't absolutely love being a mother, but it was nice to be out among the adults with no one pulling on her shirt, wanting up. *If Brice and I are together, this can potentially be a very passionate and steamy few nights away.* Instead, she knew it would be awkward and perhaps a little soul-destroying. *Brice has shown me he doesn't want me—the silent treatment usually does that—but why did he ask me here in the first place when he had no intention of speaking with me or introducing me to anyone he knows? Do I need more proof he only wants me for sex? Without Nicholas at home with us, there is nothing stopping him from taking what he wants either. And my self-control where he's concerned doesn't exist.*

BRICE DIDN'T THINK he would be spending so much of the evening talking business. First with Trent and his brothers, and now with Asher.

"The compound is ready as long as Trundaie is set."

"It's settled. From now on we will be more conscious

where we choose to do business."

"About fucking time. A last-minute change in location could have crushed B&H. If I couldn't adjust the formula to meet the difference in temperature—"

"Yeah, I know. It was close, but you called it right. Ian knew just how to handle them. Differently than I would have, but results were all I was after."

That and no bloodshed. He was glad he didn't have to be involved in the day-to-day business. He liked things he could control.

Looking around, he saw someone he had been avoiding. He was the son of one of the largest oil refineries in the US. B&H was their major competition, providing an alternate energy source and the tools to use in manufacturing. Not someone he thought would want to talk to him. "Hey, is that James West? He's been trying to contact me, but I haven't had time to talk to him yet. What do you think he wants?"

"I have no idea. While you're here, why don't you find out?"

If it was about what he thought it was, this wasn't the place. His father was far from an advocate for B&H. If James thought he was going to come into the picture to bring them down, he was sadly mistaken. *B&H isn't going anywhere.*

By the end of the evening Brice was in shock. He'd never expected Asher Barrington to propose to anyone, let alone propose publically. *I didn't see that coming.* He thought he had known him. They grew up together and neither of them had ever spoken of a family, not even once. Was it that they both had been so busy driving their business to even notice the changes within them, or were they always these guys and never wanted to accept it? *You're getting married, and I have a child.*

The moment he had laid eyes on Nicholas he knew his life was never going to be the same. Lena had demanded only one thing from him, to be there for Nicholas, not because of guilt but because he wanted to. It wasn't a ploy to lure him into their lives. She truly meant it. Brice could give him the best schools and a life that many would envy, yet all Lena wanted for their son was health and happiness. Brice knew there wasn't anything he wouldn't do for his son. He was going to ensure Nicholas had the childhood he never had. *A happy home. A father who wanted him.*

He turned and looked at Lena, who had fallen asleep in the car on the way home. She looked exquisite at the auction. Had he told her? Probably not. Brice had so much running through his mind. He had wanted to introduce her to his brothers, yet it wasn't the time nor the place. She deserved so much more than a casual introduction at an event. *I can't say, "Hey everyone, this is the mother of my child. Oh yeah, forgot to tell you, I'm a father."* He wasn't sure how he was going to approach the subject, but he knew it needed to be soon. *Very soon.*

She stirred and moaned softly, muttering his name as she slept. God, he wanted nothing more than to carry her up to his bedroom and make love to her all night, and by the look on her face, she wouldn't have objected. *Sorry baby, tonight you'll have to enjoy me only in your dreams.*

Tonight was a huge eye-opener. While watching his friends finding happiness, Sophie had cornered him and had given him an earful of what he was doing wrong and surprisingly what he was doing right. It had been a long time since anyone had given him a good pep talk. *Way overdue.* That didn't mean he believed everything she said because she was like Lena and never said anything bad about a person. *Not even someone like me.*

No, tonight he needed to be alone. His eyes had been opened. His treatment of Lena was unfair. It needed to stop, but to what extent he wasn't sure. He thought back to Trent's words: *My father told me if your life doesn't drastically change when you become a father then you're not doing it right. No one changes overnight. And some never do. But do I want to end up like my dad? Bitter, resentful, harsh . . . alone? Fuck. Surely I am allowed some happiness.* Sophie's wise words came back to him too. *You're not your father, Brice Henderson. You have been an incredible brother to your siblings. They've felt safe because of you. You're successful in business, and for that I applaud you. But don't let that hold you back from knowing love. It's there for you, too.* He just wasn't sure if she was right.

This was going to be a long restless night but until he knew the answer, he couldn't move forward. He'd addressed the past, he was finally comfortable in the present, and that left only one area of his life that needed clarification. *His future. No. Their future.*

Brice hated to do it, but there was someone he needed to talk to tonight. Contacting him at this late hour probably was unwise, but once he heard what he had to say, maybe he would be forgiven for the disturbance.

Once he knew Lena was tucked away in her bed, he went to the living room and made his call.

Chapter Twenty-Seven

BRICE HAD ACTED so differently after the auction. If she'd worried she would need to beat him off with a stick, she was sorely mistaken. When they returned to his house, he thanked her for joining him and told her to have a good night. *No kiss or hug. What the hell was that all about?*

She knew he wanted her. The way his eyes followed her the entire night said so. Even if she tried to deny it, she wanted him to take her, love her the way he had the other night. Her heart was breaking from the wedge he placed between them.

When she suggested earlier they pick up Nicholas today instead of leaving him there another night, he didn't even argue. *God, he doesn't even want to be alone with me. It's time for me to leave. I can't do this to myself anymore. Why should I?*

She called her mother and let her know they would be by shortly. "Is everything okay? You sound sad. Didn't you enjoy yourself last night?"

"It was lovely. I just miss Nicholas, that's all." *And so*

the little white lies continue.

"Everyone is here, so I guess the timing is perfect."

Oh great. The last thing I need is to see more people, especially family who know me well. Can I crawl under a rock and hide? All I want to do is return to the time when it was just Nicholas and me. Simple times. Lonely perhaps, but less confusing.

There was no way to get out of it. If she even attempted to grab Nicholas and run, they'd never let her forget it. *Maybe I should be honest with Mom, and she will cut me some slack.* As they pulled up to the house she saw all the cars were still there and realized she would never be that lucky.

Great. Don't they have anything better to do than get handouts at Mom and Dad's today? Getting out of the limo, she didn't need to knock on the door. Her mother must have been peeking out the window because she opened the door and brushed right past her and hugged Brice. *Nice to see you too, Mom.* She wasn't happy with Brice and would have enjoyed watching her mother grill him. But that didn't seem to be in the plan. *Nope, they seem to have welcomed him into the family with open arms. This is only going to make it all the more difficult later.*

Brice had never shown affection publicly before so she was surprised to see him smiling and welcoming her greeting. *Well, at least you like one of the Razzi women.*

Shaking her head, she entered the house to find the one person she knew loved her. *Nicholas.*

"Mom, we can't stay any longer. We have been here all afternoon. I want to make sure we get Nicholas home before bedtime," Lena said to her mother.

"Lena dear, Brice has never had my homemade clambakes and white chowder." Mary turned to Brice. "I'm sure you don't mind staying a few more minutes, do you?"

"Not at all. I would love to." He smiled.

Lena gave him a look of bewilderment. Last time they'd been there he'd looked for any excuse to bolt; now he was dragging his feet. He wanted to get Lena back home and back to his bed, but there were still things that had been left unsaid on his part. It had been a long sleepless night, but he knew what he wanted now. It was really what he had wanted ever since the day he had met her all those years ago. He wasn't a gambling man and solely functioned on facts. But if he had to guess, he would suspect she felt the same way about him. Everyone left and headed for the kitchen. Brice stopped Lena. "What's the rush?"

"I want to go home," she answered flatly.

"Miss me that much, do you?" he teased, trying to get her to relax.

She glared at him. "I am thinking of Nicholas."

"That's a shame," he said. "You know, Nicholas really seems to enjoy it here. Maybe I should tell Mary we're spending the night. I'm sure she would love that."

"Don't you dare."

"I thought you wanted what was best for Nicholas."

Placing her hands on her hips she stated, "Brice Henderson, I have no idea what is going on with you. Last night you barely spoke to me. You were so distant and . . . cold. Today, you are like . . ."

Tell me Lena. Like what? "Say it."

Her voice low so only he could hear, she said, "Like the old Brice. The one I used to . . . care for."

Used to. Don't you care for me now? Had his actions pushed her away for good? Was that why she wanted out of there? This was her family and she no longer wanted him to be any part of it? How could he blame her? The last few weeks he had been giving her mixed signals. He wasn't sure how she had put up with him this long. *But I'm glad you did.*

He wanted to pull her into his arms and show her how much he needed her in his life and that he wasn't going to let her go. He wasn't the old Brice, that person didn't exist any longer. But he wasn't the same person he was a few weeks ago either.

Brice wasn't letting her off the hook that easily. He knew this was only payback for what he had put her through. Last night while she slept, he had spent hours speaking with Ernest and Mary. They had a lot of questions and a few concerns as to his intentions toward their daughter. He had answered them as honestly as he could. It had taken a lot of convincing to make them see he was telling the truth. *Why should they have taken me at my word? Everyone knows my family name. Our reputation isn't something to be proud of. What I told them was the truth, and hopefully you'll see that too.*

"Mary. Ernest. Would you mind coming into the living room for a moment?" Brice asked. It was now time to share those feelings with the one person who held the answer. *Lena.*

They appeared on cue, as did her brothers and Nicholas, who was holding something in his hand. Brice reached out for his empty hand and walked him over to Lena. Kneeling down next to his son, he looked up to Lena. "Our son has something for you."

He whispered in Nicholas's ear and then he opened his hand up to Lena. Nicholas said, "Mawwe me."

Brice watched as her eyes went wide open in shock then glossed over with tears. She didn't take the ring, so he took it from Nicholas's hand. Reaching for her left hand he said, "Lena, I've been an idiot. Watching my father die while still bitter and angry taught me something. We have lost so much time; I don't want to lose anymore. Three years ago, I fell in love with you. I was a foolish man then, pushing you away. I was thinking you would be better off with someone more deserving of your love and gentleness. But when fate brought you back into my life I knew the only thing time had done was make my love for you even stronger." Holding the ring up he said, "Three years ago I said nothing was more important to me than my future. That hasn't changed. My vision of the future has changed though. My dreams are nothing if you are not by my side. If you would do me the honor and be my wife, I promise to spend the rest of my life loving you, proving to you again and again that you are, and always will be, the most important person in my life."

Lena's hand trembled and she looked around the room as though looking for confirmation, to know she wasn't dreaming. He couldn't blame her. He'd done nothing to earn her trust or her love and forgiveness. He only hoped he wasn't too late. He was willing to do anything he needed to do to convince her, his words weren't empty, his love for her was real.

After much persuasion, he was able to get her parents' blessing. Now there was only one person left, the most important one. *Lena. I don't deserve you, beautiful girl, but please take a chance on me.*

"Brice, are you sure?"

She looked at him with a wary expression. Tears were in her eyes, and he watched helplessly as a few fell over her soft cheeks. *How could I have walked away from you and hurt you so deeply? God, I'm so sorry. I promise baby, I'll never do that again.* If she took the ring and threw it at him, he knew it would be well deserved, but instead she looked at him with love, as she always had. He hadn't deserved that, but he would do anything it took to be a better man, a better friend, a better husband. He didn't want to see that look in her eyes again. He didn't want to cause her pain anymore, just the desire of her heart.

Her words echoed through him again. "Brice, are you sure?" *Never have I been more sure of anything in my life.* He stood up and cupped her face in his hands. "You are the only thing I am sure of. I love you. I love our family." He kissed her lightly then asked again, "Will you marry me, Lena?"

"I love you too. I always have. That's not the issue. I don't know if I could bear it if you—"

He knew what she was going to say. "I won't. That was a dark time in my life. I was full of anger and pushed everyone I loved away from me. I thought it was best for you. I still regret that decision. I won't make that mistake again." He'd never begged for anything in his life, but this was going to be the one exception. "Please baby, trust your heart. You know I love you. Let me give you the family you want. The family we both want."

Lena looked at Nicholas then back to him. "Yes. Brice. Yes, I'll marry you."

He pulled her into his arms and kissed her firmly. He slipped the diamond ring Nicholas had been holding onto her finger. Brice picked Nicholas up into his arms, holding him as he kissed Lena again. The flashes from Mary's camera didn't stop him. Outside of seeing his son for the first time, this was the greatest moment in his life. It was the day he let go of the past, held solely to the present, and looked forward to the future. *Their future.*

Epilogue

THIS WAS GOING to be the first of many family dinners at their home. Brice couldn't think of a better way to introduce the Razzi family to the Hendersons than over a Sunday dinner. Zoey had stopped by earlier to help Lena make everything, as the ladies said, "perfect." As far as he was concerned, the moment Lena agreed to be his wife made his life already perfect.

Although they kicked him out, it hadn't stopped him from popping his head a few times into the kitchen to make sure all was going smoothly. It shouldn't have surprised him how welcoming and loving Zoey was to her soon to be sister-in-law or her new founded nephew. Even when he told Zoey about Nicholas, her only reaction was to throw her arms around him and say "About time."

When he called his brothers and invited them to dinner, their reaction was all the same. *What's wrong?* It had been too long since any of them had gathered for the pleasure of just seeing each other. Lena had insisted that if they were going to be a family, that meant the extended family as well. She was right, and it was long overdue. Their reactions to the news was more of shock. Why shouldn't they have been. He himself had no idea how a woman as amazing as Lena could ever love him. *But thank God she does.*

They had chosen to bury their father privately as they each needed to face their pain in different ways. But now was the time to start some healing. He had a clear understanding of what he wanted for his future. He had let go of so much of the pain inflicted on him in the past. It was time the others did the same. Maybe through seeing the love he and Lena shared, they too could change the path they were on. *God knows I couldn't have done it without Lena.*

He held Lena's hand in his as he carried Nicholas in his arms. "Are you ready for this?" Brice asked as they approached the door.

"I have to admit, meeting your brothers for the first time scares me a bit, but with you two by my side, I'm ready for anything."

Brice leaned over and kissed her softly. "Trust me, Lena, they are going to love you."

"Me too. Wuv me too." Nicholas chimed in.

"Yes Nicholas, your uncles are going to love you too. Just like Daddy loves you." *I can't imagine my life without you, little man.*

Nicholas wrapped his arms around Brice's neck. "Wuv you, Daddy."

It was the first time he heard his son say those words.

It hit him like nothing he had ever experienced. Lena had given him so much: her heart, her love, and a son. His life was complete. *Except for maybe a daughter.*

"What are you laughing at?" Lena asked as he began to open the door.

"I was just thinking of a princess bed I had seen online." When she went to ask him about it, he brushed her lips again with a light kiss. "We can discuss it later in bed."

The End

Be the first to hear about my releases
jeannettewinters.com/contact.html

Other books by Jeannette Winters

Betting on You series:

Book 1: The Billionaire's Secret (FREE!)

Book 2: The Billionaire's Masquerade

Book 3: The Billionaire's Longshot

Book 4: The Billionaire's Jackpot

Book 5: Novella All Bets Off (2016)

Barrington Billionaire Series:

Book 1: One White Lie

Book 2: Table For Two (2016)

Book 3: You & Me Make Three (2016)

Book 4: Virgin For The Fourth Time (2016)

Book 5: His For Five Nights (2016)

Book 6: After Six (2017)

Excerpt from The Billionaire's Secret

Billionaire Jon Vinchi is a man with one passion: work. His friends decide to shake him up by entering him as a prize at a charity event.

Accountant Lizette Burke is dressed to the nines and covering for her boss at a charity event. She's hoping to land a donor for the struggling non-profit agency that employs her.

She never expected to win a date with a billionaire.

He never thought one night could turn his life upside down.

One lie stands between them and happily ever after. Too bad it's a big one!

Prologue

"INCREDIBLE, I NEVER knew that about him."

Still wearing their black suits from earlier that afternoon, the four men now sat in silence, silently recalling their memories of Brad from the past ten years of their friendship.

The loud crash of a waitress dropping a glass brought them back to the present. One of the men said, "I don't think any of us knew."

All four nodded in agreement.

"I still can't believe it. Only twenty-eight," another said.

"That could have been any of us in the accident."

The somberness of the moment overtook the noise of the bar. The men raised the beers they'd been nursing and said in unison, "For Brad."

✧　✧　✧

Five years later

"SO ARE YOU telling me Jon's not showing up for this

meeting, either?" Trent Davis asked as their monthly Skype meeting began. His frustration was apparent not only in his tone but in his facial expression as well. He continued, "Who knows what lame excuse he'll have this time. Maybe it's time we reconsider continuing on with this."

"Trent, I wouldn't consider you having a date with a hot brunette as a valid excuse for missing last month's meeting, either," Drew Navarro added sarcastically.

"You're just jealous, Drew," Trent stated.

Ross Whitman knew even though both Drew and Trent were extremely serious about business, they had also been equally fierce competitors in everything else they did since they'd met in college a little more than fifteen years ago. Even now, although they were all thirty-four, there were times he was convinced they were still living in their college frat house. If he didn't get them back on the issue at hand, this meeting could go on all night without them accomplishing anything.

"We've invested so much in this," Ross said. "The four of us may have started this organization, but there's no reason we can't continue building Takes One with only three of us."

Drew wasn't ready to throw in the towel on this project, or on Jon. "We have to remember why we started this." The three men thought back to Brad and his secret mission in life: to make a difference in the lives of those who were suffering, one person at a time. What amazed his friends to this day was how Brad had been able to do so much with so little money. He was the only one of them who hadn't pursued a career in big business. No one had understood why until he passed away. The day of his funeral, they'd all committed to continue with his mission in his memory. "Our objective was a priority to Jon when we started, and I believe it still is. We just have to wake him up and remind him of that fact. Anyone want to bet if I've still got the magic touch to make things happen after all these years?" He laughed. No one commented. "Wise choice, because you know you were going to lose your money." He laughed again. "Let me make some calls. I think I've got an idea that might do the trick, and if it doesn't work, then I will agree to continue what we started without Jon's involvement in Takes One."

Both Trent and Ross agreed—and were glad they weren't on the receiving end of whatever Drew was plotting.

Chapter One

J ON VINCHI SAT behind his mahogany desk, everything in order except for one piece of mail, which it seemed someone had intentionally left right in his line of vision. He could tell by the envelope it was an invitation of some sort. Matt, his personal assistant, handled all invitations for him with a standard response: a polite "Regrets, I cannot attend," and a gift or donation suitable for the occasion.

Jon buzzed the intercom for Matt. On cue, his assistant appeared at the door and asked, "Do you need something, Mr. Vinchi?"

Without looking up, Jon held out the envelope and said, "You missed one."

Matt did not reach for the envelope, instead responding, "Mr. Vinchi, that is not an invitation. It's the itinerary for the charity fundraiser that you're participating in Friday evening."

Everyone knew Jonathan Vinchi not only did not attend events, he definitely did not participate in them. Jon slid the contents of the envelope out. His eyes quickly scanned over the itinerary and stopped abruptly at his name.

"What the hell?" Jon muttered loud enough for Matt to hear. Jon brushed the itinerary to the edge of the desk toward Matt like it was an annoying fly and said, "Get on the phone and let them know I will not be there Friday."

"Mr. Vinchi, I have to admit I was surprised when I saw the itinerary as well. I placed the call first thing this morning to inform them of the error. The—"

"Good," Jon interrupted. "Then this is no longer an issue."

Clearing his throat, Matt continued, "Not exactly. Mr. Scott, the chairman of the event, informed me you had emailed him personally to volunteer."

It was unlike Matt to drop the ball. Not wanting to spend all day going back and forth on this, Jon said harshly, "Really, Matt? I personally volunteered? And you believed that load of crap?" Shaking his head in disbelief at the entire situation, he barked, "Fix it!"

"Mr. Vinchi, I have tried. Mr. Scott said they could not change the program at this late date, as the programs are already printed and in place. It's three days before the event." After a short pause, he continued. "I've tried everything, including requesting a copy of the email they stated they received from you, but everything seems to be in order."

Jon knew he hadn't sent such a request. Firmly he said, "Send it to me." Without delay Matt turned and left the office to forward the email.

Jon could not wait to see this so-called proof from the event's chairman. Once he had it, he would call Mr. Scott himself and end this charade. He wasn't going to buy any excuse about a late cancellation. This wasn't his error; it was theirs. There was no way he was participating in that event on Friday night.

The ding on his computer announced the arrival of Matt's email. He figured one quick phone call and the misunderstanding would be resolved, then he could turn his full attention back to his business, where it needed to be. Glancing quickly at the email, it looked like it came from his personal address. However, the message was signed "Jonathan Vinchi," and he never used his full name—he always used Jon. To everyone else, the email would look legit. There was no way the chairman would have known this email wasn't from him. He was furious, but the error wasn't the fault of the chairman or the event planner. Someone had gone to a lot of trouble to set him up, and he had a feeling he knew exactly who it was and how he would deal with them.

Grabbing his cell phone, he sent a text message to his three associates: "Conference call NOW!" *What the hell were they thinking?* Jon thought. He was well aware his duty to their organization for these types of events required nothing more than sending a nice donation. If his friends thought someone should participate in person, they should have submitted their own names, not his. He was too busy for this nonsense. Yesterday he had received a notice from the FDA informing him of the software changes they required. If he did not meet their thirty-day resubmission deadline, the entire project would be kicked back, and he would need to start the submission process again. The proposal had to be perfect this time. If not, he was sure his competitors would swoop in on this opportunity to launch their own devices. He had spent the last two years on this project, and he was so close—only twenty-seven days left to make all the necessary corrections. He could not afford distractions now. Too much was riding on this; his name was riding on this.

He remembered what his father always told him: "No one remembers the name of the person who came in second." These words motivated him all through high school to earn a full scholarship to Boston University, where he earned his BA and master's degrees in computer science, and then his PhD in robotics engineering at MIT. Those degrees had driven him to start his own business, Vinchi Medical Engineering, and at age thirty-four, he still lived by those words to keep the company on top.

The intercom buzzed. "Your conference call is ready on line one, Mr. Vinchi."

"What the hell were you guys thinking?" Jon barked as soon as he got on the line. Not waiting for them to answer, Jon continued, "Whose bright idea was it to submit my name to participate at this event—or any event, for that matter? This type of thing has your name written all over it, Drew. Is this your doing?"

As always, Trent said it the way it was. "If you had attended the last meeting, Jon, you would have been brought up to date for this and would have had the chance to voice any opposition to your participation."

It was a moot point, Jon knew he'd missed their last meeting—actually, their last few meetings—due to his own business needs. But this stunt wasn't solely about the meeting, and he knew it. "Trent, I have always supported the decisions you guys have made in the past, but I am not supporting this one. What makes you think I will even show? I don't have time for this nonsense."

"Time is valuable to all of us, Jon. We all have our own companies to run besides supporting what is needed for Takes One. Either you're fully invested in this, or you're not. There are times when it takes more than sending in a donation, and this is one of those times. When we started Takes One five years ago, we committed to doing this kind of work. Yes, there are the donations we grant anonymously, but the organization is about so much more than that, and you know it," Trent said.

Jon knew Trent wasn't only talking about this event. He was referring to Brad and how fully invested he had been in this type of work.

Ross said, "Takes One has never been about us. There are a lot of people who benefit from it, Jon. Friday night is about what our organization can do now and in the future."

Once again, these were all facts Jon already knew, but at the moment Ross's comments weren't helping. Their timing to pull this type of shit couldn't have been worse.

Drew added, "There's no way to retract your participation Friday night. It's only one night of your life—actually, just a few hours. Let's get through this event. We can save the rest of the discussion about the future of Takes One for our next monthly meeting."

Jon knew it was true—there really was no way to avoid his participation without tarnishing his own name and making the people he was ultimately trying to help suffer. But he was far from through discussing this issue. Jon said, "Trust me, Drew, I will be on the next call and we can discuss your involvement in this setup in more detail." Whatever his friends and colleagues were up to, he wasn't going to be a pawn in their game. It used to be fun betting who could outdo whom with some outrageous prank, but he had left those days behind when he graduated college. You don't have such luxuries when you're the owner of a business. At the end of the day, everything rides on you, and you stand or fall alone.

He hung up the phone with more force than necessary. He picked up the itinerary once again.

Charity raffle to benefit: Fight Against Hunger
Entrance donation: $10,000
Three door prizes. Top prize: A Date of Your Dreams With Billionaire Jonathan Vinchi

His eyes never made it to the other prizes. He could read the itinerary a thousand times, but the fact would never change: He was being raffled off. A mix of anger, frustration, and disgust flowed through him as it became apparent that no donation was going to get him out of this.

God, he did not need this type of distraction. Not now, not ever, but especially not at this critical time. It was going to be a long week.

THANK GOD IT'S *Friday,* Lizette thought as she rubbed her temples, trying to ease the dull headache that had been haunting her for the past two hours. She wasn't sure if it was all the system issues she'd faced while trying to process the month-end accounting report or something else, but today had felt like it would never be completed.

Taking one last look at her desk, she confirmed it was tidy as always, with everything in its place. *Almost over,* she thought as she shut down her laptop.

Getting out on time on a Friday was a great way to start the weekend. Lizette had her entire weekend planned out. She had so much to do, but Friday night was all hers. It was dedicated to relaxing. During lunch she'd made sure to download the latest steamy romance onto her Kindle. She could not contain her smile thinking soon she'd be soaking in a hot bubble bath with her novel and a glass of wine, enjoying a well-deserved escape.

Her sweet thoughts were interrupted by the ringing of her phone. The clock showed 4:59. *Why does the phone always ring at the last minute?* She sighed. Lizette contemplated not answering it, but then the caller ID lit up with the name Elaine Manning. Elaine was the CEO of her company, Another Chance, and Lizette knew she couldn't avoid taking the call. Since they were all friends in the office there was also a chance she wasn't calling about business.

"Hello. Lizette Burke speaking. How may I help you?"

"Lizette, I'm glad I caught you. Can you come to my office right away?" It was a question that had only one answer.

"Certainly, I'll be right there." There was obviously something wrong with the month-end report. "So much for that bubble bath," she said quietly to herself.

Lizette quickly adjusted her blouse and smoothed her fitted skirt. With one quick look in her compact she confirmed her hair was still in place, in a tight bun secured with a pencil.

She made her way through the all-too-quiet hall and headed to the executive office. The door was open and Elaine motioned her in. She was on the phone, rapidly firing instructions for a limo and a dress. Elaine attended many social functions in the hopes of gaining financial support and sponsorship for Another Chance. From the sound of it, she must be attending an extravagant one this evening, because she never used a limo.

At age thirty-four, Elaine Manning was known for her beauty and poise. But today her jet-black hair was in disarray, her nose red, her eyes bloodshot, and her cheeks flushed. Her entire appearance screamed "fever." It appeared she was the latest victim to succumb to the flu that was making its way through the office. If Lizette had known earlier she would have brought her some soup. It was clear, she needed to go home and go to bed. There was no way she should be attending anything for a few days.

Even though she felt bad Elaine wasn't feeling well, all she could think of was getting out of this office as she had been lucky enough to avoid catching it and could only hope her luck wasn't about to run out. *Please make this quick so I don't get sick too.*

When Elaine hung up the phone, she said, "I hope you don't you have plans this evening, Lizette."

Oh, great. Something big had gone wrong with the report. Everything appeared to have gone too smoothly. She had been handling the books for Another Chance for the past five years, and this was the first time it went off without a hitch. Lizette should have known better. She knew it. This was going to be an all-nighter. She knew whether she had plans or not, her answer needed to be the same. "No, my evening is free. Is there a problem with the month-end report? I will be happy to stay as long as it takes to correct whatever issue there is." Lizette took her job seriously—too seriously, some had told her.

Accurate accounting was the foundation of a company, she thought.

Elaine grabbed more tissues just in time for a sneezing fit that seemed to go on forever. Seeing her so ill, Lizette relented and thought, *Whatever she needs, I'm happy to help her.* Whatever the issue with the report was, Lizette was confident she could handle it on her own.

"No, no, the report was fine. I need you to do something else for me, for the company."

Lizette could not even guess what that could be. All she'd ever done was accounting but she was a team player, so whatever office work needed to be done, she would try her best. "Of course, I am an excellent typist. Did you need me to fill in for your administrative assistant while she is out sick too? You know I'm more than happy to do whatever I can."

"Thank you, Lizette, I do know and appreciate your dedication. However, it's not her role I need you to fill tonight. It's mine."

Hers? she thought. *As CEO? I would not feel comfortable having to make all those critical decisions. I like numbers; they're factual, they don't lie, they're black and white, no gray areas.* And yet, it was Friday night; there really couldn't be anything that would come up that couldn't wait until Monday. She could do this. All she'd need to do was be on call for anything critical. Then it hit her: Maybe there was something critical going on she wasn't aware of. Maybe there was a fire in the community or something. Lizette didn't have to wait long to find out.

"There is an extremely important event I was supposed to attend this evening. Obviously I am too ill to go."

That was clear from the moment I entered the office, but what does this have to do with me? Lizette wondered.

"I need you to go in my place," Elaine continued, pausing to sneeze again. "To represent me, represent us, Another Chance."

Lizette hoped Elaine couldn't see the shock and horror that was surely written all over her face. Even though she and Elaine were similar in some ways, the major difference was Elaine carried herself with such confidence she could walk into any room and hold her ground on any topic even with the most influential people. That was not something Lizette enjoyed or was interested in doing. "What? Oh, no, I couldn't . . . I can't . . . you know I don't . . ." Lizette didn't even realize she was stumbling over her words. She did not want to attend such a high-profile Who's Who event. That was the last place she wanted to be.

"Lizette, there is no one else who can do this for me tonight. You know my admin Jill is home sick, and the rest of the team is on vacation or also out sick. We need you to do this." After another sneezing fit, she continued, "I need you to do this. You're head of the accounting department. I don't have to tell you what attending an event like this can do for our association. It's a great opportunity to get our name out there. The people attending could provide exactly the type of funding we need to continue. Normally we could never afford to attend, but an old colleague of mine, Mr. Scott, is the chairman of the event and was kind enough to sponsor a ticket for me. Someone has to represent us. We won't get another opportunity like this."

Lizette knew it was true. All the recent cuts in government funding had hit nonprofit organizations like Another Chance extremely hard. Right now they were basically running on personal donations and barely making it. It was getting crucial to find a corporate sponsor; the future of their organization was at risk.

"It's one night. All the arrangements have already been made. The dress is being delivered to your home at six o'clock. The limo driver will pick you up at seven thirty, and Mr. Scott has been told you will be representing me—I mean, us—tonight."

As though Elaine noticed the writing all over her face, she continued. "Lizette, this is not only an important charity event, it's our best shot at networking with people who can provide the kind of financial support we need. I would not ask you to do this if I didn't know you would represent us well." In a softer voice, she went on. "We've known each other for several years now. I know you can do this. Do what comes naturally. Talk about what you believe in. Talk about the business and all that we do. Tell them about some of our successes. I know you are passionate about what we do here, so it'll be easy. You'll see." With a sincere smile she said, "You may even enjoy yourself so much you'll wish you could do it all the time."

Doubt it, Lizette thought. Yet there was no way to get out of tonight after the speech she'd just received. She knew Elaine was not asking this of her as a friend; she was asking as the CEO. When the CEO asks for a favor, especially one of this magnitude, you don't really have the option to decline. "Thank you. I will do my best," she said with a forced smile.

"I need to get to bed. Thank you for filling in for me tonight." Ms. Manning's eyes traveled over Lizette's very conservative business attire as she said, "Better get going, Lizette. You have a lot to do before seven thirty."

Don't remind me, she thought as she rose and left the office. She felt bad Elaine was ill, but for once she wished there *were* problems with the month-end report. At least she knew she could fix that. An event like tonight's was something she wasn't comfortable with, something she had been able to avoid since her college days—until now.

*Look for a linked series set in the same world, written by Ruth Cardello (my sister).

You won't have to read her series to enjoy mine, but it sure will make it more fun. Characters will appear in both series.

Available Now (FREE!)

Books by Ruth Cardello

The Legacy Collection:

Book 1: Maid for the Billionaire (available at all major eBook stores for FREE!)

Book 2: For Love or Legacy

Book 3: Bedding the Billionaire

Book 4: Saving the Sheikh

Book 5: Rise of the Billionaire

Book 6: Breaching the Billionaire: Alethea's Redemption

Book 7: A Corisi Christmas Novella

The Andrades

A spin off series of the Legacy Collection with cameos from characters you love from that series.

Book 1: Come Away With Me (available at all major eBook stores for FREE!)

Book 2: Home to Me

Book 3: Maximum Risk

Book 4: Somewhere Along the Way

Book 5: Loving Gigi

Recipe For Love, An Andrade Christmas Novella

The Barringtons

A new, seven book series about the Andrade's Boston cousins.

The first series in the Barrington Billionaire WORLD.

Book 1: Always Mine

Book 2: Stolen Kisses (Available for Pre-order)

Book 3: Trade It All (Coming 2016)

Book 4: Let It Burn (Coming 2016)

Book 5: More Than Love (Coming 2016)

Book 6: Forever Now (Coming 2016)

Book 7: Never Goodbye (Coming 2016)

Excerpt from Maid for the Billionaire
Book 1 of the Legacy Collection

By Ruth Cardello

Available at all major eBook retailers for FREE!

Dominic Corisi knew instantly that Abigail Dartley was just the distraction he was looking for, especially since having her took a bit more persuading than he was used to. So when business forces him to fly to China, he decides to take her with him, but on his terms. No promises. No complications. Just sex.

Abby has always been the responsible one. She doesn't believe in taking risks; especially when it comes to men – until she meets Dominic. He's both infuriating and intoxicating, a heady combination. Their trip to China revives a long forgotten side of Abby, but also reveals a threat to bring down Dominic's company.

With no time to explain her actions, Abby must either influence the outcome of his latest venture and save his company or accept her role as his mistress and leave his fate to chance. Does she love him enough to risk losing him for good?

Chapter One

BY DYING NOW, his father had won again. *That old bastard.*

Dominic Corisi slammed the door of his black Bugatti Veyron and stepped onto the sun baked Boston sidewalk without giving the million-dollar vehicle a backward glance. The joy of owning it was dead along with his desire to answer the incessant ring of the cell phone he'd ignored since yesterday. Rather than turning it off, he'd muffled the noise by burying the device deep within a coat pocket, maintaining the connection to his life like a distant beacon.

Despite the oppressive heat, he paused at the bottom stair of his old brownstone. There was nothing spectacular about it, outside of its location near the upbeat Newbury Street. If he remembered correctly, its rooms were small and the main staircase had a creak that he never did get around to fixing. It was nothing like the sprawling mansions he now owned in various countries around the world.

But it was the closest thing he had to a home.

His phone rang with a tone he couldn't ignore. *Jake.* His second in command would simply call again, killing whatever chance Dominic had of finding a moment of peace inside those brick walls. "Corisi," he barked into the phone.

"Dominic, glad I caught you," Jake Walton said smoothly, as if he hadn't unsuccessfully rung twenty times in the last two days. That was Jake, calm and professional, even in the storm of hostile takeovers. Nothing fazed the man.

Normally, Dominic appreciated his even temper, but today it grated on him. Maybe the forty or so hours without sleep were beginning to catch up with him. He fought an impulse to toss his phone over the metal railing. The world wasn't the orderly, rational place Jake liked to organize it into. It was messy. It was ugly. And, most recently, it lacked justice.

"How is Boston?"

The inane question almost sent Dominic over the edge. "How do you think?"

It was probably too much to hope that Jake's uncharacteristic silence signaled an end to a conversation Dominic wished he had avoided.

"We need to discuss the China contract. The Minister of Commerce is expecting to meet with you tomorrow to cement the details. This is your dream, Dominic. By next week, Corisi Enterprises will be a major global player. What do you want me to tell the minister?"

"I don't know," Dominic said wearily.

Jake made a sound somewhere between a choke and a cough, then was speechless—a revealing response for a man who handled irate international diplomats without missing a step. He was the fixer and navigated the unexpected with ease. Until now.

Poor Jake. Nothing in their shared history had prepared either of them for Dominic's sudden desire to withdraw from the world. The creators of financial empires didn't take sudden vacations and they most certainly didn't hide, especially not after having laid the groundwork for the single greatest business venture of the century. Bill Gates himself had called last week to discuss the ramifications of the negotiations.

"Jake, I need to drop off the radar for about a week. Why don't you take over the China contract?"

"Okay . . ." Jake said awkwardly. In another situation, Jake's loss of composure would have been amusing.

"Can you handle it or not?" Dominic challenged. He could barely think past the throbbing of his headache.

Maybe coming to Boston was a mistake. It had been here, at seventeen, that he'd walked away from his inheritance and waited tables to fund the search for his mother. Here, in this very brownstone, that he'd cultivated a hatred for a father who had denied both involvement and interest in the disappearance of his wife.

Jake's voice slammed Dominic back into the present. "No problem. I've followed the progress you've made with the Chinese Investment Promotion Agency. They're eager. I'll clear my schedule and cover yours. Duhamel will forward all of your calls to me until further notice."

"Good."

"Dom . . ." Jake hesitated. "It's normal to need time to grieve. You just lost your father."

A harsh laugh escaped Dominic. "Trust me, I'm not grieving his loss." He leaned a hip on the metal railing and looked up at the building he had instinctively returned to, searching for the man he'd once been and hoping to find something there that would shake off the immobilizing apathy he felt for all he had done since—high expectations for brick and antique wallpaper.

Jake said, "That's what worries me. No matter what your plans were or what he once did to you, he's gone now. You've got to let it go."

Jake was asking the impossible. Of course the past mattered. Sometimes it was the only thing that did. "Just do your job, Jake. If you can't handle it, tell me and I'll promote Priestly to help you."

For the second time since they had met at Harvard, Jake lost his temper. "That's bullshit, Dom. You want to send Priestly to China? Send him. You're absolutely right—you've made me a very rich man. I don't need this. But heed my warning: you won't be a billionaire for long if we both step away from the helm. A lot is riding on this contract. The lawsuits alone will freeze your assets if you screw this up. You invested too much of your own and you're playing with the big boys now. Governments are not very forgiving when it comes to last minute walk outs."

The speech should have shaken Dominic, but it barely breached the numbness that had settled in since he'd received the phone call from his father's lawyer. What did all the money matter anyway? He'd wasted fifteen years amassing an empire that would allow him to throw down a forced buyout contract on his father's enormous mahogany desk. Dominic should have taken action years ago, but no level of prior success had felt like enough. He'd choreographed the day from both sides, building his company while undermining his father's, always working toward that one absolute win. Dominic had counted on his father's desperation finally forcing him to confess what had actually happened to his mother.

It was that loss he mourned today.

In its place was a carefully orchestrated set of instructions from his father's lawyer. No, it wasn't enough to simply disinherit his only son—Antonio Corisi had also included provisions in his will to ensure that Dominic had to attend the reading. He'd used Dominic's one weakness, his one regret, to reaffirm his control, even from the grave.

Jake coughed, reminding Dominic that a response was required. What could he say? As usual, Jake was correct in his assessment of the situation. Dominic had used his own wealth as well as that of his investors to back this venture. The risk had seemed worth it. The government contract would crack China's software market wide open for them while their global influence would double exponentially. It was a daring move that, if carefully implemented, could put Corisi Enterprises on a stratosphere of power few companies ever acquired—a goal that a week ago had seemed imperative.

Jake could handle the negotiations. Dominic had always been the one to charge forward, shaking the situation up and clearing the way. This time would be no different. Jake would merely take over a few documents earlier this time. Priestly was good at the local level, but he was no Jake.

"One week, Jake." It was the closest to an apology Dominic was able to get out. He hoped it was enough.

Sounding more like an older brother than a business associate, Jake said, "Take two weeks if you need it. Just get your head together. I can wrap up the China contract, but it'll need your final signature and your presence. I'll do a press release today and ask the media to respect your need to mourn in private; that should give you at least a few days before they descend."

"Call Murdock." *The man owes me a few favors.*

"Do you mean the Murdock? I thought he'd retired."

Ah, there is the real difference between us. By not fighting in the trenches of financial warfare, Jake's business associations had remained above reproach, but he lacked the backdoor connections to those seemingly innocuous individuals who wielded real international influence. Dominic casually gave Jake a number that many would have paid a small fortune to dial just once. "Men like Murdock don't retire, they delegate from warmer climates. Tell him I don't even want a good spin on this. It's non-news. He'll understand."

Jake whistled softly in appreciation. "Is there anyone you don't know?"

"Yes, you if you call me again today."

Jake laughed, but they both knew it hadn't been a joke. "Do yourself a favor, Dom . . ." Jake continued in an unusually authoritative tone.

What now? Dominic sighed.

"Put down the Jack Daniels for a night and pick up one of those models you like to date. You'll sleep better."

Dominic gave a noncommittal grunt and hung up. *If only it were that easy.*

Chapter Two

ARMS FULL OF bed linens, Abby Dartley froze at the click of the front door opening. *Darn it.* She couldn't get caught here, especially in an oversized shirt and jeans instead of her sister's maid uniform. *Lil needs this job.* Cleaning the brownstone of a man who never actually occupied it had sounded like a relatively simple, albeit annoying, way to help her sister remain employed.

"Do not let anyone see you," Lil had pleaded between the fits of sneezes that had accompanied her low, but persistent fever. "They'll fire me in a second if they find out you went in my place."

"Can't you just call in?" Abby remembered suggesting hopefully.

"I already used my two allowed sick days for Colby." And then the tears had come.

A year ago, Abby would have let her sister add this lost job to the long string of employment she'd already tried and failed at and would have covered her expenses until she found a new job. They'd been through this cycle countless times, resulting only in Lil resenting Abby more with each passing year. The closeness they'd shared before the death of their parents was a distant, surreal memory.

Abby had considered asking Lil to move out, hoping that some separation would give Lil the independence she said she wanted, but that was before she'd held her new niece in her arms. It wasn't just about Lil anymore. Colby deserved a mother with a stable career and Lil was so close to having one. She was one semester from finishing her administrative assistant courses. Even when Colby's father had walked out at the news of his fatherhood, Lil hadn't crumbled. For the first time since they'd received the news of the accident that had claimed the lives of both their parents, Lil wasn't hiding from her responsibilities.

Colby had changed that, too.

It wasn't Lil's fault she'd caught the flu. Half the city seemed to be either recovering from it or succumbing to it. More importantly, it had been a long time since Lil had actually requested help, rather than merely grudgingly accepting it. Abby didn't want to put too much significance on such a miniscule connection, but she couldn't shake the hope that things could get better between them.

Her first impression of him as he stood in the entrance, unaware of her existence, was that he looked more tired than a man his age should. Dark circles were evident even against his olive complexion. His expensive suit did nothing to conceal the slump of his wide shoulders. According to Lil, he'd paid to have the brownstone cleaned on a weekly basis, but hadn't actually been there in over a decade. Something had brought him back and whatever it was, it had steamrolled right over him.

He looked up and through her as he crossed the foyer. "You can go now."

She considered following his weary command, but something held her immobile.

"Are you deaf? I said you can leave. Finish whatever you're doing tomorrow."

Mr. Armani sounded like an overtired child, although she was fairly certain he wouldn't appreciate the comparison. The wisest choice of action would have been to do as he said and leave before he had a chance to question her attire, but she couldn't.

He didn't look like someone who should be alone.

Was she simply projecting? Her friends often accused her of seeing good where there was none, but that was a hazard of her job. To be an effective middle school teacher, one had to see beyond the bravado. Abby taught English to non-native speakers, so she was often employed in the toughest schools in the city. She was used to defusing misdirected anger. Profanity was a cry for help. Harsh words often hid fear. Her patience paid off. Students returned, year after year, to thank her for believing in them. For some, she knew she'd been the only one who had. But this wasn't her classroom and, in reality, she had no idea who this man was.

She could almost hear Lil's voice telling her some

things were simply not her business and she'd be right. This man wouldn't welcome her nurturing any more than her sister did, but that didn't stop Abby's heart from going out to him.

She put the sheets on a table on one side of the hallway and said, "There are fresh towels upstairs. Why don't you go take a shower and I'll get some basic groceries from the corner store for you."

His back straightened and she caught her breath, reeling from the full impact of his attention. *God, he's beautiful.* His dark gray eyes raked over her, flashing with irritation and then something else. He cut the distance between them in a few short strides. A hint of alcohol reached her as he stopped mere inches from her. She tipped her head back to look up at him.

"Did Jake send you?" he asked as he assessed her. "You don't look like a model."

She blinked a few times in surprise as some of her sympathy for him faded. "And you don't smell like a man who should be wearing an Armani, but I wasn't going to mention it," she answered in a huff.

Her words must have stirred something in him; his shoulders squared and his eyes narrowed. This was a man who was not accustomed to people speaking back to him, but if he was trying to intimidate her, his nearness was creating the entirely wrong reaction in her body. Even in his rumpled suit, or maybe because of it, he was the sexiest man she'd ever seen in person. Men like this existed only on the large screen or in novels. She wanted to reach up and run a hand over the rough stubble on his cheek.

"I didn't say you were unattractive," he growled. "You're just not reed thin like the women I'm used to."

That's it. She put her hands on her hips and raised her eyebrows in a silent challenge.

Time suspended as their standoff continued. His look of annoyance was steeped with an expectation that she should try to appease him some way. She simply met his glare with her own, giving him time to replay his choice of words in his mind. He looked away first, a slight flush reddening his neck.

"Okay, that came out wrong." He ran a frustrated hand through his thick black hair, leaving it slightly awry and sexier . . . if that were even possible. He was already a twelve or thirteen on her one to ten scale, even after she deducted a few points for lack of social skills. A glint of fascination lit his dark eyes as something occurred to him. "Did you just tell me that I stink?"

There was nothing tired about the way he leaned down until their lips almost touched. The scent of him mixed with the dash of liquor and the combination was heady. He was all male, untamed and interested in more than her answer to his question. No man had ever looked at her with such intensity. His sexual energy demanded a response that her body seemed all too willing to deliver.

Abby fought down the urge to close the short distance between them. She'd lost too much to believe in anything that felt this good. She took a half a step back and raised a placating hand. "I wasn't quite that harsh."

The corners of his mouth twitched in amusement. "Do you have any idea who I am?" he asked, somehow making the question sound more curious than pompous.

Perhaps his tragedy had brought him a bit of notoriety, but Abby wasn't one to watch much TV and, as usual, Lil had given her just the information she absolutely needed in a brief, stilted conversation that typified how strained their relationship had become.

"I'm hoping you're the man who owns this brownstone, otherwise I'm going to get in trouble for letting you in," she said with some forced humor.

He didn't laugh. "You really don't know, do you?" His question sounded oddly hopeful.

Abby shrugged, but the hairs on the back of her neck tingled. What kind of man was relieved not to be recognized?

A criminal.

Crap.

Nice clothes meant nothing. His suit might have become disheveled during a tussle with the actual owner of it. She shook her head at the thought. "You do own the place, don't you?"

At his lack of a response, she scanned the area for something to toss at him if she needed to dash for the door. The closest object was a large, brass lamp. If he made any fast moves . . .

All coherent thought fled when he smiled down at her while lightly running his hands up both of her arms.

"Yes, I'm the owner."

Her heart really shouldn't be pounding in her chest just because the man was preparing to restrain her if she attacked him with deadly, brass force. It wasn't like she'd never been near a man before, but even her prior intimate relationships had been cautious endeavors. No man had ever brought to mind the words *carnal abandon* like this one did. When he looked at her, no one and nothing else existed.

"Before you clock me, would you like to see my license?" he asked while his thumb traced the edge of her collarbone rhythmically. Hypnotically. "Would you?" he prompted in response to her silence.

"Yes," she said breathlessly, unable to concentrate on anything beyond the way her body was responding to his touch. Her skin burned beneath his light caress. Her stomach quivered with an anticipation she had previously only read about. *Yes, to whatever you're asking.*

Her state of arousal was not lost on the man towering above her and the answering pleasure in his eyes shook her out of her daze. She stepped back, away from his touch and gave herself a mental shake. This kind of passion had no place in the life she'd built for herself. "I mean no. No, I believe you. You were right. I should go. I can finish everything tomorrow."

His lids lowered slightly, making his expression unreadable.

"Do you know what I'm thinking?" he asked.

Unless he was also imagining the two of them naked, rolling around on the thick area rug in the living room, she was pretty much stumped. "No," she croaked.

"I'm starving and I hate to eat alone. I'd be grateful if you joined me for a meal."

That wouldn't be wise. There were at least a hundred, maybe a thousand, reasons why she should leave now before she made a fool of herself. Yet, she was tempted.

It was more than the athletic span of his shoulders, more than the strong line of his jaw. She couldn't even blame the sadness in his eyes, because the exhausted man of earlier had been replaced by a virile male who knew exactly how to get what he wanted—and right now he wanted her.

Every sensible cell in her body urged her to turn tail and run, but wasn't that what she always did when life offered her something she considered too good to be true? She chose safety and certainty over less reliable dreams and desires.

Just this once she wanted to sample what she'd been missing. Just this once she wouldn't run.

Well, not immediately, anyway.

She'd share a meal with the near god before her, enjoy the way he made her skin tingle with just a look, and leave before anything happened. He wouldn't have to eat alone and she could have an hour or so of pretending any of this was real.

"Any problems with Chinese?" she asked as she mentally reviewed the local places she knew would deliver.

The question seemed to jolt him. "Chinese what?"

"Food?" she added helpfully.

"Oh," he visibly relaxed. "Takeout."

"Yes, there is a good place right around the corner that I know delivers—unless you'd like me to try to find something else."

"No." He shook his head at some private joke. "Sorry, for a minute there I forgot." Hands in his pockets, he rocked back on his heels, still looking highly amused by his thoughts.

"Forgot what?" she couldn't help but ask.

With unexpected tenderness, he slid one of her wayward curls behind her ear. "That you're exactly what I need." Before she could catch her breath, he stepped back and handed her far too much money, no matter what she ordered. "Order some food while I take a shower." His knock-'em-dead sex appeal returned as he chuckled and sauntered away, tossing over his shoulder, "I've heard I need one."

Abby fanned her red face with the bills as she watched him climb the stairs two at a time. Not quite shaking herself free of the mental image of Mr. Armani naked beneath the steamy spray of the shower, Abby went in search of her purse and cell phone.

A man that sexy is just trouble.

Luckily it was unlikely that she would ever see him again after today. They would share one quick meal and then she'd head back to Lil and reality.

Back to the quiet, predictable life she'd built for herself.

That thought held less appeal than usual.

Available now!

65687117R00158

Made in the USA
Charleston, SC
05 January 2017